Marital Advice
to my Grandson, Joel

How to be a husband your wife
won't throw out of the window in
the middle of the night.

Marital Advice
to my Grandson, Joel

How to be a husband your wife won't throw out of the window in the middle of the night.

Peter Davidson

SWEET MEMORIES PUBLISHING

A Division of Sweet Memories, Inc.

sweetmemories@mchsi.com

This book is based on the author's personal experiences and his imagination. Any resemblence to other real persons or other real events is purely coincidental.

ISBN: 978-0-692-99815-1
Library of Congress Control Number: 2017919313
First printing, January, 2018

Published by Sweet Memories Publishing

PRINTED IN THE UNITED STATES OF AMERICA

10 9 8 7 6 5 4 3 2 1

Acknowledgments

Editor: Wordright Services

Graphic Design: Debbie Wilson

Front Cover Art: Jason Tako, Debbie Wilson

Back Cover Photo: Jessica Ann Photography

Reader: My wife, Beverly, who was the inspiration
for this book.

Dedication

This book is dedicated to my grandson, Joel, and his wife, Abby,
in honor of your marriage.

Abby - you're perfect as you are—don't change a thing.

*Joel - you're a guy, and you can use all the advice
and wisdom you can get.*

Peter Davidson

TABLE OF CONTENTS

Hidden Truths About Marriage

Joel, to your wife, Abby, you will be more than just a husband – you will be a *Project*, a *Work-in-Progress.*

When Abby chose to marry you, she apparently saw in you hidden potential that no other woman in the world was able to spot, including her mother, her sisters, and her friends. For the rest of Abby's life, she will try on a daily basis to coax, mold, and beat that hidden potential into some semblance of the admirable man she visualizes you have the ability to become.

This epistle is a guide for how to understand, accept, and fulfill your role in the marriage and how to understand, at least a little bit, what makes your wife tick.

Advice is given on topics such as – make sure you buy a roll of electrical tape before you volunteer to do the vacuuming – and why, how to interpret Abby's steely-eyed, clinched-jaw scowl, known as "The Look," how to properly answer Abby's questions such as, "Does this dress make my ass look big?," and how to create the world's most powerful anniversary card for your wife.

You will be wise to use these words of wisdom to self-train yourself so you can lessen the amount of training that needs to be inflicted upon you by your wife. With the wisdom provided in this epistle, some nudging from Abby, and a few of your own ideas, in no time you will become the magnificent man that Abby always thought you had the potential to be.

Hard to Believe –
You a Married Man!

I started writing these pages of profound marital advice two days after you got engaged. It is my hope that this wisdom will help you to avoid many of the potential marital landmines that will attempt to bombard you throughout your life.

MARITAL WISDOM, PASSED DOWN FOR GENERATIONS

Prior to your getting married, some well-meaning friends, your brother, your dad, an uncle, some cousins, and even strangers will take you aside and try to explain what married life is all about. I know this, because before I got married to Grandma, a whole bunch of self-styled philosophers offered me marital wisdom and advice. Believing everything they said, I wrote down their wisdom so I could refer to it often for guidance and direction. Even though these gems of wisdom were given to me several decades ago, they are just as true today as they were back then and they will be just as true many years from now as well. There is no time limit on truth.

So, here is that timeless wisdom and advice for you to study, contemplate, ponder, and digest. Since some of the advice is quite deep and philosophical, I have added a few comments in parenthesis, based on my years of marital experience, just to help you out a bit.

- "It takes a lot of effort to make a marriage work." (That advice, by the way, is like giving you a rowboat somewhere off the coast of California, pointing out into the ocean and saying, "If you paddle in that direction you'll eventually reach Hawaii.")
- "Women are a lot different than men." (Really?)
- "Marriage can either be Heaven or Hell." (Makes sense, no?)
- "Keep your powder dry." (I've had 40 years to think about this comment and still don't know what in the hell Uncle Fred meant by it.)
- "Be careful what you confess to in a weak moment – women have a memory like an elephant." (Every married man on earth has found this out first hand.)
- "Just treat her like one of the guys." (You might contemplate this advice carefully before you teach your wife how to cuss, chew tobacco, and spit.)
- "When it comes to other women, look but don't touch." (Dah)
- "Measure twice and saw once." (The purveyor of this fabulous wisdom was a carpenter, but in marital terms it probably means you should think twice before you open your mouth.)
- Your wife will not see the humor in your introducing her to others as your *'First Wife.'*" (No shit.)
- "Just when you think you've got your wife figured out, she'll run a reverse on you or throw a Hail Mary." (This advice came from my high school football coach –

profound.)

- "Your wife is allowed to say low-down, mean, nasty things about her mother, but you are not." (It's a mother-daughter thing that you'll never understand. Philosophical question for you to contemplate - what if you actually like her mother, are you allowed to say nice things about her?)
- "Even if you have a headache, don't turn her down if she wants to have sex." (Brilliant advice, from a guy named Bubba.)
- "The key to a successful marriage is to always pick up your socks off the floor." (Great advice, but it's not quite that simple.)
- "Be careful, or she'll turn out just like her mother." (Egads! But, fear not – it's only true 57% of the time.)
- "Break only one law at a time." (This advice could apply to many things, but in marriage I think it means you should not forget your wife's birthday and your anniversary in the same year.)
- "If you whisper another woman's name in your wife's ear, or shout it, particularly during a moment of passion, there is no way to lie your way out of it, but give it a try anyway." (This advice came from a guy who spent three years sleeping in the basement.)
- "Never play poker with her father or throw darts with her brother." (The guy who told me this never said why, but I think her father had been playing poker for thirty years and her brother had been throwing darts for ten

years and they both kicked his ass and subsequently labeled him a loser.)

- "Your wife-to-be is beautiful, built, smart, and nice – marry her quick before she gets onto what a loser you are." (Joel, this advice would apply to about 95% of the guys out there, but not to a couple of smooth guys like you and me.)
- "It's a sin to mess around with other women, but a crime to get caught." (From one of the great philosophers of our time.)
- And, finally, a word of wisdom from your Grandfather: "Your mouth will get you into a whole lot more trouble than your *Willy* ever will." (From the voice of experience.)

What would a man accomplish
if he were to become rich and famous
and conquer the world,
if he didn't have the love of his life at his side
to share the journey.

THE WEDDING PLANNERS

Abby has been making plans for her wedding since she was eight years old. Her mother has been making plans for this wedding since your wife-to-be was three months old. You started seriously thinking about the wedding two days ago. You may be at a little disadvantage here. Fear not – I have advice for you.

Setting the Wedding Date

The first step in planning a wedding is to set the date. If this has already been done, you can skip to the next section because it is too late for the following advice to be of any value to you, unless by some miracle you are able to convince Abby, and her mother, that the date should be changed. Good luck with that.

If the wedding date has not been set, however, here is where you need to do your best to stand your ground – Do Not get married on a Saturday or Sunday during football season. If you do, half of your buddies will refuse to attend and the half that do show up will be mad as hell for your idiotic choice of a wedding day.

If you would have had the good sense to consult with me before you even asked the love of your life to marry you, I would have suggested that you somehow work into your marriage proposal the stipulation that the wedding could not take place on a Saturday or Sunday during football season. Most likely, Abby would have been in a euphoric mood when you *popped the question* and she would have readily agreed.

So, if you're getting married on a Saturday or Sunday during football season, that one's on you.

Planning the Wedding

In your wedding, in any wedding, the bride is the focus of attention and the star of the show. Your role, as husband, simply, is to show up, to look nice, and to repeat the words, "I do," on cue. And that's it. Period.

In fact, if it were possible to have a proper wedding without the groom's being there, some brides would do it. However, they actually do need you, so you'll be a part of the show but keep in mind that your role is that of a bit player, because the starring role has already been taken.

When it comes to planning the wedding, your role is simple – stay out of it. Nobody, and I do mean *Nobody*, gives a damn about your opinion on how this wedding ceremony should be conducted. This includes Abby, her mother, her sisters, and all of her friends. If your own mother has been invited to be a part of the wedding planning, she doesn't give a damn about what you think, either.

Oh, out of courtesy, Abby might ask for your opinion on a minuscule item or two, just to give you the illusion of being involved in the planning. If you express an opinion that is contrary to what she has already decided to do, she'll do what she was planning to do anyway. So, try to find out which way the wind is blowing and jump on the bandwagon. Or, better yet, when she says, "Do you think we should . . . ." give her the one answer that you'll eventually find advantageous to use in multiple situations throughout your entire married life, "Yes, Dear."

Your Specialty – the Party

Now, all of the foregoing advice may have been for naught because you probably don't give a hoot about how the wedding ceremony is conducted anyway. Likewise, your buddies will not remember a thing about your wedding ceremony, unless it is unbearably long, the bridesmaids are smokin' hot, or you pass out at the altar.

What you're interested in, and what your buddies will remember, is the party after the wedding. Here is where you can show your stuff and get involved and Abby will probably allow you to have some input, just as long as you keep your mitts off of the Main Event.

Just like any other party, the after-wedding party will be a huge success if there's plenty of cold beer, booze, food, and some kick-ass music. Cheers!

Planning the Next Wedding

Some twenty or twenty-five years from now, you may have the wonderful opportunity to be involved in another wedding – that of your daughter. There are only two things that you need to do here.

The first is to ingrain in her, starting when she is about four years old, that she can have her wedding any time that she wants, but not on a Saturday or Sunday during football season. Your buddies and your future son-in-law and his pals will admire you for this wonderful foresight.

Your second role in your daughter's wedding is simple, it is to *P-A-Y*.

Settling Into Married Life

The first few months of married life are a time of adjustment for both you and your wife. You may think that you know Abby and what makes her tick, but you are wrong, my friend, wrong.

In many ways, it is easier to adjust to the BIG things involved in living together than it is in adjusting to the small things. Read on for some examples that are loaded with profound wisdom and advice.

COMPATIBILITY OR COMPROMISE

On many day-to-day issues, Abby and you will be in full agreement and will be totally compatible, which is wonderful since it causes no controversy or dilemma for either one of you. There will be other issues, however, where the two of you are not in agreement, which will result in your needing to work out a compromise. Here is a simple example:

In your bathroom is a roll of toilet paper on a holder. Now, the paper can either roll over the top, or roll under the bottom. If you are both top rollers or are both bottom rollers, no problem – perfect compatibility. But, if one of you is a top roller and the other is a bottom roller, you have an issue with the tissue. And, this is not a small issue, since you will both come face to face with it several times a day and if the paper rolls the wrong way, it will irritate you, or Abby, each and every time. No shit.

This is where compromise is going to be necessary. The two of you just can't go on switching the toilet paper from a top roller to a bottom roller and back again every time either of you hits the John.

Most likely, the reason you are either a top roller or bottom roller is because that's the way it was in your parent's home and that seems the way it's supposed to be. The same is true of your wife; it's a family tradition.

So, we have now identified the problem, but have not come up with a solution, so far. As previously stated, you cannot go on forever, each switching the toilet paper to match your top roller or bottom roller preference; you need to settle on one method and stick with it.

It is hereby recommended that you give in to Abby's preference, but there are potential rewards for you as well. For one thing, it will serve as a powerful incentive for you to work hard to become successful enough to have your own bathroom where you can roll the toilet paper as you damn well please. For another, think of the fun you can have when Abby's family comes to visit and you switch the toilet paper from her family's roller preference to your own. It will completely puzzle and bewilder them and, for a moment, give them the impression that it is you who is running the show, albeit a false impression.

Happy rolling!

*As the Marital Bus rumbles
down the highway of life, there cannot be two people
wrestling for the steering wheel, or surely
the bus will crash. Know when it is your turn to
drive, and when it is time to quietly sit in the back seat.*

SHARING

You learned as a child that it is good, proper, and nice to share with others. This concept carries over to marriage, but it works a little differently than it did in kindergarten.

Let's say, for example, that you like to occasionally eat a banana. You realize that Abby is not as fond of bananas as you are and rarely eats them. You stop at a convenience store on your way home from work and they have some great-looking bananas for sale. You buy two of them - one for today and the other one for tomorrow.

You get home and place your bananas on the kitchen counter. After dinner, you decide to have one of your bananas for a snack. Your wife asks, "Can I have the other banana?" Of course, you graciously say "Yes." There goes tomorrow's banana.

A few days later, you stop at the same convenience store and they again have some great-looking bananas. You decide to get yourself two of them – one for today and the other for tomorrow. You recall, however, that last time you did this, Abby ate your second banana. You decide to compensate for this and buy three bananas; two for you and one for your wife.

You get home and place the three bananas on the kitchen counter. After dinner, you decide to have one of your bananas for a snack. Abby does not ask if she can have a banana.

The next evening, after dinner, you decide to have your other banana as a snack. Abby still does not ask if she can have the remaining banana.

By the third day, Abby still has not asked if she can have

the remaining banana. By this time, it has turned black and is inedible. You throw it out in the garbage.

Like I said, sharing in a marriage is not the same as sharing in kindergarten. Good luck figuring it out.

Just think – of the billions of men in the world,

your wife chose you.

That's how special she thinks you are.

Make it your life's mission to prove her right.

MOMMY'S LITTLE HELPER

When you were a child, remember when your mother would occasionally give you little tasks to do, such as "Please go in the living room and bring me the red pillow from the couch," or "Get me a tissue from the box on my dresser," or "Hold this bowl for me until I need it." Maybe you were even rewarded for your help by being allowed to lick the batter from the mixing bowl beaters.

Your Wife's Helper

Well, you're a big boy now and your wife is going to occasionally call upon you to run some simple errands for her. For instance, say you're in the grocery store and Abby gives you an order: "Go get the smallest box of oatmeal they've got. It's in the cereal aisle."

You charge off and locate the cereal aisle in less than ten seconds. The oatmeal is in the first section on your left. You're making good time. And then you see it – a stash of oatmeal boxes and canisters taking up an area seven feet high and ten feet wide. Seventy square feet of oatmeal.

There is strawberry oatmeal, blueberry oatmeal, maple oatmeal, cinnamon oatmeal, raspberry oatmeal, original oatmeal, brown sugar oatmeal, one-minute oatmeal, and a whole lot more. There are square, rectangular, and round containers ranging from a few ounces to several pounds.

You remember your instructions, "Get the smallest box of oatmeal they've got." You look them over and there it is – the smallest box of oatmeal on the shelf and you grab it.

You rush back to where you left Abby in the frozen food section and, of course, she is gone. After searching the entire store and having come to the conclusion that she has been kidnapped, you finally find her – she has doubled back and is in the canned soup aisle. You proudly hand her the box of oatmeal that you have so carefully selected.

Abby scrutinizes the box, gives you a bewildered look and says, "I can't use raspberry oatmeal in my meatloaf recipe." And she charges off toward the oatmeal section at high speed. No licking the batter from the beaters for you today.

Fool Me Once, Shame on You – Fool Me Twice, Shame on Me

You are now expecting sage advice on how you should have handled this situation, and you shall get it.

First Strategy: In the future, try to never again go grocery shopping with your wife.

Second Strategy: If the first strategy doesn't work, try to stay as far away from your wife, and the grocery cart, as you can, so you cannot be sent on impossible missions like hunting for oatmeal.

Third Strategy: If the first two strategies don't work, ask for specifics of exactly what size, color, and shape the box is, what the brand name is, if there are any special requirements, such as Original, Instant, Powdered, or . . . .

About the time you get this far with trying to get an exact description of what you are to go fetch, your wife will be so disgusted with you and so impatient that she'll roar off to go get it herself.

She'll get over it, and you weren't going to get the beaters to lick anyway.

Mommy's Helper – the Truth

When you were a kid you probably screwed up every task your mother gave you to do, too, but she was too kind to tell you what a f*ck-up you were because, even though you didn't realize it, you were in the early stages of your lifetime of training to be a husband.

Blasting Down the Aisle

Here's one final shopping tip for you. On occasion, Abby will ask you to stop by the grocery store to pick up a few items. The store will be packed with other shoppers and the aisles will be damn near impassable because of shopping carts blocking your way. Some shoppers have the uncanny ability to block an entire aisle all by themselves by strategically placing their cart in the exact middle of the aisle and they won't budge for nothing.

This is a little trick that I learned years ago and it works every time. Not all shopping carts are equal. Some have nice, perfectly round wheels that roll smoothly and silently down the aisle. Other carts have received a good deal of wear and abuse and some of the wheels have flat spots on them that make a Boom-Boom sound as the cart wheels down the aisle. You might think that you should select a good-conditioned shopping cart with smooth wheels, but you are wrong, young man. Select a shopping cart that has at least two wheels with flat spots on them – three or four wheels with flat spots would be even better. When you come charging down the aisle, your cart will sound like a steel-wheeled lumber wagon on a brick highway – Boom-Boom-Boom-Boom-Boom-Boom-Boom-Boom-Boom. Other shoppers will hear you coming two aisles away and they will jump out of your way and you will have the aisle to yourself with a clear path to the checkout counter. Works every time—Boom, Boom, Boom.

Money can buy almost anything,

but it cannot buy the love of a good woman.

BRAGGING RIGHTS

There are few things that some married women enjoy more than getting together with other wives and having a full-blown bitching session about what a bunch of low-down, miserable, worthless, lazy, sloppy, gross, crude, barbaric idiots their husbands are.

There is one thing that a wife likes better than that, though. It is being able to brag on her husband to her friends and relatives about the wonderful things that he does to help out around the house. That being the case, take the lead here and get out in front of it. That is, pick two, three, or four things to do around the house that will surprise and please your wife and astound your mother-in-law.

Your New Best Friend

I highly recommend that one duty you volunteer to handle is vacuuming the carpets and floors. Here's why: There is something about the hum of a vacuum cleaner and knowing that her husband is the one running the machine that gives a wife a euphoric high that borders on having a mental orgasm. In fact, some women have reported that they consider their husband vacuuming the floors to be a form of foreplay. That might inspire you to vacuum four or five times a week.

Here's a little tip – before you start vacuuming, go to the hardware store and buy a roll of electrical tape. Why? Because sooner or later you are going to run the vacuum over its electrical cord and the vacuum will gnaw the outer casing off the cord, exposing its bare wires, which, eventually, will cause the cord, and maybe the house, to catch on fire. Here's where the electrical tape comes in. All is not lost, though. When your wife brags to her friends and relatives that you do the vacuuming, fully three-fourths of them will not believe her. She will then show them the vacuum with its taped-up electrical cord as physical proof that you do, in fact, vacuum. You see, women do not vacuum over the electrical cord. It's a guy thing.

Here's one final vacuuming tip: Abby will expect you to move the clothes hamper, wastebasket, bathroom scale, and other objects sitting on the floor and to vacuum behind them. From a guy's point of view, this is overkill and most likely you won't move them and vacuum behind them every time that you vacuum. So, occasionally, move one of those items and leave it sit in the middle of the floor, as though you forgot to put it back. When Abby sees it sitting there, she'll be impressed, believing you have done a thorough job of vacuuming.

Adding to Your Repertoire

Find two or three additional things that you can handle that don't take too much of your time and add them to your list, like taking out the garbage, shaking out the throw rugs, and occasionally washing and/or wiping the dishes.

One final thing that you will be well advised to add to your list of domestic skills is cooking. You don't have to become a chef or anything like that, but find one thing – just one thing – that you can cook that you become famous for in your household. It can be anything – scrambled eggs, spaghetti, French toast, homemade ice cream topping, or grilling burgers. It doesn't matter what it is and the only requirement is that it be reasonably edible.

The Extra Touch

As a final touch when you are doing your vacuuming, window washing, cooking, or whatever, whistle while you work. Your wife will interpret this as a sign of your contentment and she is sure to tell everyone what a happy warrior you are. And, when she hears you start to whistle, she'll break into a smile. Look what you did – you made her happy!

Accolades

Abby probably won't tell you this, but when she brags to her friends and relatives about what a fantastic volunteer you are around the house, they are bound to tell her, "He's quite a catch."

Ya, that's you they're talking about. And it's a whole lot better than being the object of a good ol' fashioned bitching session.

*A woman gets married when
she finds the man of her dreams.*

*A man gets married when
he wakes up one morning and says to himself,
"I think it's time to get married," and he does –
to the first woman who will have him.*

BEDROOM BLISS

You probably think this is going to be about sex, and it is – in a roundabout way. More directly, it is about farting. Farting in bed. There is probably nothing that will disgust your wife more than your cutting one under the covers. Oh, I know – you think that your farts are both silent and odorless. *Wrong* and *Wrong again.*

At first, you might be able to get away with slipping a few little ones past your wife without being detected, but it won't last forever.

Farting Etiquette

It is improper etiquette for you to refer to your farting as *Tooting.* Women *Toot,* but men do not. Men *Fart.* It is important that you understand this distinction.

Becoming a Fartaholic

You may not know this, but farting in bed is much like becoming an alcoholic. You see, a person who eventually becomes an alcoholic doesn't start by guzzling a quart of gin on the very first day they have their very first drink. No – they have a cocktail or two and it tastes good, but that's all they have. Then, slowly, they increase their consumption over a period of time until they work up to that quart a day – a full-blown alcoholic.

Farting in bed is the same thing – you start with a little blooper that goes undetected and then you get bolder and bolder until you become a full-blown *Fartaholic.* Eventually the night will come when you let loose with a *Five-Alarm Ripper* that rattles the windows and causes your wife to go sleep on the couch for the rest of the night. This is where you should "take the cure," just as a drinker does when they finally have to admit to themselves that things have gotten out of control.

The Seven-Alarm Bomb

If you do not take control, you may end up like Sammy – and this is a true story that actually happened to one of your Grandpa's beer drinking companions. Sammy started out by slipping a few silent ones past his wife. As his flatulence gradually became more noticeable, his wife protested and threatened to no avail.

Sammy kept blasting away under the covers. Then, one night, Sammy let a sauerkraut salad and bean burrito-fueled *Seven-Alarm Bomb* that was so massive, deadly, forceful, and lethal that it set off the carbon monoxide detector in the bedroom.

Sammy, of course slept through it, which left it up to his wife to turn off the detector, that was screaming like a police car siren. She was afraid to turn on the light switch for fear a spark would blow up the house and eventually she fumbled with the detector in the dark until she got it turned off.

After that night, Sammy was relegated to sleeping in the guest bedroom, which is where he still sleeps to this day. And, it is hard to have sex with your wife when you are sleeping thirty feet from where she is sleeping and you have been banned from her bedroom at any time of the day or night.

Taking the Cure

So, to make your wife happy and to improve your sex life, go to the drug store and buy a bottle of those little pills with names like *The Fart Blaster* or something like that, which provides an instant cure to being a bedroom fartaholic.

Sweet dreams.

Be careful what you confess to in a weak moment –

women have a memory like an elephant.

"DOES THIS DRESS MAKE MY ASS LOOK BIG?"

There will be numerous times throughout your married life that your wife will ask for your opinion on how she looks. Here's an example.

Abby and you are getting dressed for your company's annual holiday party. Abby purchased a new dress for the occasion and she will wear it for the first time tonight. She views herself in the mirror – front, side, and rear views.

"Does this dress make my ass look big?" she asks.

This is a *trap question*. If you answer it wrong, your wife will burst into tears, will rip the dress off, and probably refuse to go to the party. If she does go, it will ruin her entire evening – and most likely yours as well. Not only that, but she will remember what you said forever and will throw it back in your face at least once a month for the rest of your life.

Now, there is no doubt that you consider yourself to be one of the most quick-witted and funniest guys on the planet. Humorous quips pop into your mind such as, "Naw – it's no more than two ax-handles wide," or "Don't worry about it – it's all behind you."

Here are three thoughts for you to consider:

First, you're not as funny as you think.

Second, you're walking on eggshells here.

Third, this is a wonderful opportunity to deliver a superb compliment to your wife that she will deeply appreciate and that she will remember for a long time, if not forever.

It doesn't actually matter if the dress does, in fact, make her ass look big. That's not the issue here. The issue is your saying something to soothe her concerns and make her feel good.

So, get that silver tongue of yours oiled up and say the words she needs to hear. Something like, "My Dear, you have a magnificent posterior and this dress does nothing but compliment it perfectly." Oh Gawd!

"Do You Like My . . . ." Scenarios

I will now demonstrate my mystical clairvoyant powers by predicting your answer to two scenarios similar to what your wife will ask you hundreds of times during your marriage.

Answer to Scenario Number One: "I like it!"

Answer to Scenario Number Two: "It looks great!"

Keep those answers in mind. Now for the scenarios.

Scenario Number One: Abby goes to the hairdresser and gets a new hair style. She comes home and models it for you and asks how it looks. Your answer is, "I like it!"

Even if you think it looks like her hair was cut with a lawnmower or weed eater, the answer is the same, "I like it!"

Scenario Number Two: Abby goes shopping and comes home with a new outfit. She models it for you and asks how you like it. Your answer is, "It looks great!"

Even if the color makes her look like a ghost and the pattern and design makes your eyes spin, the answer is the same, "It looks great!"

Liar, Liar Pants on Fire?

So, am I encouraging you to lie? Absolutely not. Beauty

is in the eye of the beholder, and in your eye it is beautiful and "It looks great!"

What would be gained by telling your wife that her haircut looks like it was cut with a chainsaw or that her new outfit makes her look fat? Nothing. And, it will only upset your wife and probably make her mad at you for saying such mean and spiteful things.

But, don't you have a responsibility to tell your wife the truth? Well, truth, like beauty, is in the eye of the beholder and we know that in your opinion the truth is, "It looks great!" and "I like it!"

Oh, Oh - the Truth

Your wife will eventually learn the truth about her new hairstyle or her new outfit, and it will come from a more experienced and more reliable source than you. This is where your wife's mother, sisters, and friends come in. It is their responsibility to tell her the full, complete, and unadulterated truth. Sooner or later, one of them will level with her. And, when Abby comes home downhearted and says that her good friend told her that the new haircut looks awful, you can comfort her by saying, "I liked it and I thought it looked great!"

Sharing Your Opinions

Here are two last thoughts about rendering your opinion on your wife's hair style, clothing, appearance, and other matters. You have already dodged a bullet by telling her "I like it!" or "It looks great!" instead of telling her the gosh-awful truth.

Remember my previously-rendered marital advice about how your mouth will get you into more trouble than your *Willy* ever will? Well, don't go spouting off to your pals or anyone else about your wife's horrible haircut or how her dress made her ass look a mile wide – it will undoubtedly get back to her and you'll have some tall explaining to do.

The final thought on rendering your opinion to or about your wife is this – don't, unless she asks for it.

*When you get married, the concept of "sharing" is a little
more complicated than it was back in kindergarten.
You can never go wrong, though,
by giving your wife the biggest half.*

"THE LOOK"

Let's say Abby and you are out for the evening with friends, enjoying a few drinks and dinner at a nice restaurant. Everybody is having a great time and it might be said that you are the life of the party.

You glance at your wife, who is sitting across from you, and she is giving you "The Look." It is a steely-eyed, clinched-jaw scowl that means you have obviously done something very wrong, but what?

It could mean, "Stop staring at the waitress's boobs," "Stop staring at the waitress's ass," "Stop talking so loud," "Stop talking with your hands, they're waving all over the place," "Stop swearing," "Stop telling the same stories that you've told these people a dozen times," "You have again spilled steak sauce on your shirt," "You are getting shitfaced drunk," "Stop crushing your empty beer cans against your forehead," "Stop yelling 'Go Big Red' every time someone in a red shirt walks by," "You have been ignoring me," "Stop winking at the cocktail waitress," "You bought the last three rounds, let that tightass buy the next one," or, "I'm bored and want to go home." Or, it could be something else.

Most likely, since there are so many possibilities of infractions that you might have committed, you are not going to figure it out. But, you don't have to. Within thirty seconds of when Abby gets you alone in the car, she will inform you.

You are told this little story to prepare you for the inevitable. All wives give their husbands "The Look" from time to time and you'll probably never know what you did to trigger it until it is explained to you in no uncertain terms. You can try to not do it again, but you're a guy, so good luck with that.

*Always remember Grandpa's marital advice:
"Your mouth will get you into a whole lot more trouble
than your Willy ever will."*

SHUT UP AND EAT IT

Maybe Abby can cook; maybe she can't. If she's a good cook, I have no advice other than for you to enjoy her culinary delights and to offer her sincere compliments on her fine cooking.

If your wife has not yet mastered the art of cooking, some diplomacy will be in order on your part. This is where my advice of "Shut up and eat it," comes in.

Even though you're a real joker, resist the temptation to give Abby a cookbook and a fire extinguisher as a gift. Your wife can make fun of her cooking and criticize it if she wants to, but not you. If all else fails, you can always fire up the grill or take Abby out for dinner.

The same "shut up" advice goes for your wife's other domestic skills, or lack thereof, including cleaning, dusting, washing clothes, ironing, decorating, and so on. Just remember, you didn't marry Abby because of her domestic skills. You married her for her wonderful personal traits, her companionship, and the love and joy that the two of you share. As long as you don't have to use a shovel to make your way through the house, who gives a damn about her housekeeping.

By the way, if your wife is struggling with some of these activities, read Page Four of the MARRIAGE HANDBOOK, which says, "The concept of *MEN'S WORK* and *WOMEN'S WORK* went out the window about the time women started burning their bras." If you didn't catch the drift, it means the vacuum cleaner, broom, and scrub brush will fit your hand just fine.

Your wife will scream twice
when you flush the toilet within eight feet
of where she is taking a shower.
The first time she screams will be when
your flushing steals the cold water from her mix and
the hot water hits her.
The second time, she will scream louder,
when she figures out that you're the cause
of what made her scream the first time.

GOOD TIMING

Here is a true story you might learn something from: Matthew and Sherry have been married for over a year and one of their biggest controversies deals with time. Matthew believes in "precision timing," which means arriving at an event precisely as it begins. His idea of arriving to church on time is that his ass should hit the pew at the same split second that the organ goes "Deeeee" to kick off the first hymn.

Sherry's idea of timing is to arrive well in advance of the start of an event so she can survey the layout of the room, pick the best seat in the house, go to the restroom a time or two, and watch other people as they arrive.

Warped Senses of Time

How did these two people end up with these extreme perceptions of time and timing? Well, when Matthew was a child, his parents were always the first ones to arrive at an event. They would arrive at church about an hour before the start of the service and they would sit in the car until at least a half dozen other carloads showed up; then they would go in. If they went to an event to be held at the 4,000 seat high school gymnasium, you guessed it – they would be the first ones there, sitting in the car. That's what shaped Matthew's *last-second, precision-timing* sense of time.

When Sherry was a child, her family was always late for everything. If they went to a movie, the main feature would already be underway as they stumbled around in the dark trying to find seats without sitting on someone else's lap. If they went to an event to be held at the 4,000 seat high school gymnasium, you guessed it – they would be the last ones there and would end up sitting in the nose bleed section or standing along the wall because all the seats were taken. That's what shaped Sherry's *get-there-early* sense of time.

The people that we're referring to about having "warped senses of time" are not Matthew and Sherry; it's their screwball parents.

Some people grow up to be exactly like their parents. Because their parents were so extreme in how they viewed time and timing, however, Matthew and Sherry each vowed to never be like them, and they turned out the opposite of their parents. End of psychology lesson.

Even though you and Abby are not Matthew and Sherry described in this story, there is a high likelihood that you are very much like them when it comes to your individual attitudes toward time and timing. Therefore, I shall make the following astute observations and suggestions.

Synchronization

Before you go scrambling for a dictionary, I'll tell you – synchronization is the process of bringing two elements together at the precise same moment in perfect harmony. Some people refer to as being "in sync." In other words, getting you and your wife to the same place at the same time, and liking it.

Here are our suggestions:
- I know that you already thought of setting your wife's

clock back a half hour, but that won't work, so scratch that idea.

- I know that you thought about lying to your wife about the starting time of an event, telling her it starts later than it actually does. This will work only once, so scratch it as a long-term solution.

- I know that you have thought about taking two different cars to an event. She can go ahead and grab a couple of seats; you'll get there when you get there. Not a bad idea. It's an even better idea if your wife goes on ahead with a like-minded friend to save some seats and you and a like-minded buddy show up later on.

- Perhaps you and your wife can go your own separate ways to your own events on your own time schedules. Your wife can go to her events with a friend and you can go to your events with a buddy. Could work, once in a while, anyway.

- Since your wife thinks about time the same way your parents do, maybe they can go to events together. Since you think about time the same way her parents do, maybe you can go to events with them. Wait a minute – going to events with each others' parents? What an idiotic idea. This ain't gonna work.

- Most of the above ideas have a fatal flaw – somehow, you and your wife are not going to these events together, and you should.

- Ah, the solution: Why don't you split the difference. Compromise. You agree to go 15 or 20 minutes earlier than you want, and Abby can agree to go 15 or 20 minutes later than she wants, and you can go together. You'll each give a little and both gain a lot. Have fun.

I know that by now you have come to expect brilliant, mind-boggling suggestions and solutions from me, but in this case, this is the best I can do. Live with it.

If you want to show your wife your charming side,
read to her from a book of poetry or
inspirational quotations.
Don't overdo it, though,
or she'll think you're up to something.

THE GIFT HORSE

There will be numerous times throughout your marriage that you will buy Abby presents for her birthday, wedding anniversary, Christmas, Valentines Day, and other occasions. Buying the perfect gift is an art and a science. If you do this right, Abby will brag to her friends about the wonderful, thoughtful gift you gave her and may even treasure it forever as a keepsake. If you do it wrong, you will pay in ways that you cannot even imagine.

I could provide a list of ten things to do and not do when buying gifts for your wife, but the following true story might be easier to remember.

A Gift She Will Never Forget, Nor Will He

It is Bill and Diane's first wedding anniversary. They have a lovely dinner at home and share a bottle of good wine. Now, it is time to open the gifts that they purchased for each other.

Bill opens his gift first. It is the golf putter that he has been dropping hints about for the past two months.

Now, Bill leads Diane into the living room where he had placed a huge box that he had wrapped personally.

With great anticipation and a big smile on her face, Diane slowly unwraps the box – and comes face to face with the most magnificent vacuum cleaner that money can buy.

Of course, Bill expected Diane to say something like, "Thank you, Bill. This is something that I can use every day of the week and I will think of you every time that I use it. This was so thoughtful of you."

What Diane did say no doubt wiped that goofy smile off of Bill's face.

"Why in the hell didn't you give me a scrub brush, broom, and dust pan while you were at it? Let me explain how this works, Bubba. Buy me flowers, candy, jewelry, clothing, perfume, a card, or nothing at all – but do not ever buy me an implement of work as a gift."

Did you get the message, Big Fella?

If you're already married, you can skip this advice
because it's too late to do you any good.
If you're not yet married, this is for you:

DO NOT

get married on a Saturday or Sunday
during football season

LET THE TRAINING BEGIN

Joel, this concept was already expressed in this epistle's introduction, but I repeat it here just in case you missed it the first time.

To your wife, you are more than just a husband, you are a *Project* – a *Work-in-Progress*.

When Abby chose to marry you, she apparently saw in you hidden potential that no other woman in the world was able to spot, including her mother, her sisters, and her friends. For the rest of your wife's life, she will try on a daily basis to coax, mold, and beat that hidden potential into some semblance of the admirable man she visualizes you have the ability to become.

You will be in training every day of your married life. Sometimes, the training will be so subtle that you may not even know you are being trained. Other times, there will be no doubt, such as in the preceding story, "The Gift Horse."

Jump-Starting Your Training

In order to make Abby's job of training you a little easier, and to give you a head start as a trainee, I offer the following tidbits:

- You probably didn't know this before, but you soon will – your eyebrows are too bushy and should be trimmed and you are growing hair on your ears that needs to be plucked.
- Whenever you wash your hands or shave, you are splashing water all over the mirror. Wipe it off.

- Your favorite jeans - the faded ones that fit just right – are not suitable to be seen in public unless you wear them to a football game or a honkytonk.
- You talk too loud when you're on the telephone, especially when you talk to someone who is in another city. Sure, they're a long ways away, but that's a damn poor excuse.
- You eat your meals like you're in a food-eating contest. Slow down.
- The television is too loud, and don't claim that they turn up the volume during commercials.
- When you talk, your hands fly all over the place; stop it before you injure someone.
- You tell the same stories to the same people over and over and over again. Once is enough.
- You grab your dinner fork like it's a hammer handle.
- Your favorite underwear, the ones with a hole in them, will no longer be acceptable to wear.
- Your buddies are welcome to drop by anytime, provided you give your wife a two-hour advance notice.
- When you get a few drinks in you, you become a real motormouth. Put a sock in it.

Now, you might think that the preceding comments and suggestions should be construed as nagging or criticism. They are not – it is *Training*. Get used to it – it has only just begun. And, after you get properly trained, you will be one magnificent specimen of a man.

UNDERSTANDING YOUR WIFE, AND OTHER MYTHS

Joel, let's say that through your keen sense of observation and your powers of intuition, you develop the ability to anticipate your wife's every mood and foresee her every action to the point where you completely understand her. What would I say about that, you ask. Well, I would say that you are an idiot and a fool who is prone to hallucinations and that you should either be examined or executed.

FEMALE SHOPPING LOGIC

Since the beginning of time, mothers and grandmothers have passed down shopping philosophies, strategies, and techniques to their daughters and granddaughters. The young women accept these morsels of wisdom as absolute, indisputable truth since they came from Mother, or better yet, Grandmother. By the time you met the woman who eventually became your wife, these truths had become ingrained in her personal DNA.

In some families, it is a ritual that is as sacred as celebrating Christmas, Thanksgiving, or Independence Day – a grandmother taking her granddaughter shopping on her sixteenth birthday. Granddaughter is now of the age, maturity, and mental capacity to comprehend the complexities of female shopping logic, as shared by Grandmother. It goes something like this:

"If you find something on sale at a deep, deep discount, buy it, even if you don't need it or have no use for it. And when you get married, if your husband cannot understand this simple logic, tell him to go f*ck himself."

That's what you're up against. Don't fight it.

*Every day of your married life will be an adventure,
particularly on those days that the two of you
never even leave the house.*

THERE'S NO STOPPING THE SHOPPING

If you haven't figured this out by now, it's time that you face the facts – men and women view shopping differently.

How a Man Shops

When a man goes shopping for a new pair of shoes, he walks into a shoe store where he has previously purchased shoes or he goes to a store that is easy to get in and out of. He looks over the shoes on display, selects a style that he likes and checks to see if the store has a pair in his size. He may or may not try on the shoes. He takes the shoes to the counter, pays for them, and heads for home where he has important things to do like watch a game on TV or do a little woodworking. Approximately seven minutes will have lapsed from the time he entered the store until he exited it.

He will wear that pair of shoes for at least ten years and the older they get the better he will like them.

How a Woman Shops

A woman will enter a shoe store and look at every pair in the store, including styles that she would never consider wearing. She will find several pair that are "perfect" and she will try them on in her size and in the sizes larger and smaller than her size, just to be sure. Then, she will leave the store empty handed and will repeat the same routine in every shoe store in the mall and in a couple of stores across the street.

Four hours later, she will return to the first store and buy the first pair of shoes that she tried on. There is a strong possibility, after expending this amount of time and effort into finding just the right pair of shoes, she might never wear them even once. Why? It is one of life's great unsolved mysteries.

A second possibility is that, after shopping for four hours, hitting fifteen shoe stores, and trying on three dozen pairs of shoes, she goes home with nothing because she "Couldn't find a thing."

Shopping Together

The reason that I feel compelled to explain this difference in shopping procedure to you is that when you were dating Abby, before she was your wife, you were probably so eager to hang around her that you would have walked through fire just to be with her. In your lovelorn daze, you would have done anything just to be with her and you probably did not even realize that you were on a shopping trip. And, she probably liked having you around.

Now that you're married, it's time for you to look at shopping more realistically – there is no way that you can go shopping with your wife. Four hours to buy a pair of shoes? Or to go home empty handed?

The good news is that Abby has undoubtedly figured out the same thing – having you tag along will put a serious crimp in her shopping style. Or, put another way, now that you're married, trying to go shopping with each other will drive both of you stark raving mad.

So, here's the deal. When you go to the mall together, you shop your way and let Abby shop her way. Take a newspaper or a book along to fill the three hours and fifty-three minutes of waiting time. Join the other burned out husbands sitting on the benches or couches scattered around the mall but do not engage them in conversation – they're in no mood for small talk.

You might set a place and time to meet your wife to go home from the mall, but this is a foolish and futile thing to do since her shopping is not governed by a time clock. You may have noticed that most women's clothing and shoe stores are like casinos – there's not a clock in sight. They don't want to even give a hint that time matters or that it may be time to go home.

Simply put, your wife will not be ready to go home until she is "done shopping."

So, just let her shop 'til she drops and then help her carry the packages. Be happy! Finally, you are on your way home.

Here's a simple idea that will save you
a great deal of grief and misery:
Buy a large twelve-month calendar, the kind with a
large square for every day of the month.
Then, jot down on it your wife's birthday, your wedding
anniversary, and any other special days.
Oh, and then look at the calendar every once in a while.

"LOOK AT THAT!"

This will happen to you dozens of times throughout your marriage so pay close attention on how to handle it with aplomb.

Abby and you are having lunch at an outdoor sidewalk cafe. You are sitting across from each other, facing one another. Suddenly, Abby looks past your shoulder and exclaims, "Look at that!"

You whip around to see what is going on behind you. There are at least fifty people, three dogs, two cats, twenty-five vehicles, a hot dog vendor, a news stand, a bus, three trucks, a policeman, two taxi cabs, ten retail stores, a hotel, two bicyclists, and a whole bunch of other stuff within your vision.

"At what?" you ask, being unable to spot anything particularly notable.

"That!" she says.

You look harder, trying to see it. You don't.

"What?" you again ask.

"Too late; you missed it," she says in disgust.

"What was it?" you ask.

"It doesn't matter now," she says, still pissed off at you for missing it.

You may think that you handled this as well as you could have and that it was unfair of your wife to expect you to play an instant game of "Where's Waldo?" with that huge scene in front of you. It doesn't work that way.

All your wife was trying to do was to share with you a

little slice of American Pie that had unfolded before her eyes. She wanted you to experience it, too.

You are eagerly waiting for a few kernels of wisdom on how to handle this situation, and ye shall receive it.

It really doesn't matter if you see that thing you're supposed to be looking at. The world will go on the same whether you see it or not. What matters is that your wife perceives that the two of you have shared an experience for a brief moment. So, give it to her.

All it will take is a well-chosen word or two that seems to confirm that you have indeed spotted what she pointed out to you, and you appreciate her pointing it out. All you have to do is say something like, "Wow!," "Well, I'll be!," "Gosh!," "Ha!," or "Holy Smoke!"

That should do the trick.

*When your wife says, "Dear, will you help me . . . . ,"
she doesn't mean next month, next week, tomorrow,
or when the game you're watching is over.*

She means NOW.

*So hop to it and get it out of the way and then you
can peacefully return to what you were doing.*

YOUR WIFE, THE ENTREPRENEUR

You may not realize it, but somewhere inside your wife is a budding business entrepreneur. Maybe she already has the bug, but if not, it will only take a comment or two to give her the fever.

Perhaps Abby is having coffee with a couple of friends when someone says, "Did you hear that Mary had a garage sale and made $800." Another friend chimes in, "Jenny had one and made over $1,000."

That is all it will take and the entrepreneurial seed will have been sown. Why, if Mary and Jenny could make $800 or $1,000, surely she could do as well, if not better. Cash money!

The Business Plan

Here is how a garage sale, also known as a lawn sale, yard sale, and by other names, works. A woman goes through her closet and selects blouses, slacks, dresses, coats, shoes, and anything else that she believes she can get along without. Then she goes through the entire house, searching for anything else that she thinks will sell. This includes old purses, appliances, furniture, décor, books, musical instruments, collectibles, and anything else that is not nailed down.

The next step is to mark all these items at a price that is enticing enough for them to sell. Perhaps $6 is a fair price for a silk blouse, $12 is a good price for a pair of nearly new designer jeans, and $4 is suitable for the lamp. The fact that the silk blouse cost $80, the designer jeans cost $130, and the lamp cost $75 does not enter into the equation. This stuff is gonna sell, Baby, sell, and she's gonna make cash, cash, cash!

You are recruited to locate folding tables, card tables, saw horses, boards, clothing racks, and anything else you can get your hands on to hold all of the merchandise.

Planning for the garage sale may take three or four weeks but the final three days prior to the sale and the two days of the sale are particularly intense. During this five-day period, you will be eating sandwiches instead of real meals because the Entrepreneur is too busy with the business to do any cooking. That's fine – she's on a mission.

Open for Business

Finally, the moment has arrived and the Entrepreneur is about to launch her business. At precisely 8 a.m., the advertised starting time of the sale, she opens the garage doors and a flood of people who have been standing out there since 7 a.m. charge in looking for bargains. Apparently, your wife wrote one hell of an advertisement for the local newspaper.

People are buying stuff like crazy and your wife is stashing cash in her metal cash box and slipping a few $20's into her jeans pockets. The experienced garage sale goers are determined to not pay the asking price - "$6 for a silk blouse – too much. Will you take $4?" They negotiate and your wife is happy to settle for $5.

As the day goes on, your wife is watching which items people look at, handle, fondle, and then put back without buying. Maybe they are priced too high and she makes a mental note to drop the price before tomorrow.

Out of desperation to sell things, your wife might even do what Jenny did to sell a purse. The purse was leather with a whole bunch of metal bangles on the outside - beautiful. It originally cost $155, but Jenny had it marked at $10. Dozens of people picked up the purse, looked it over, and then to Jenny's amazement, put it down without even making an offer on it. Jenny marked the purse down to $8, then $6, then $3, and finally to $1.50. Still, no one stepped up to buy the purse. Then, inspiration hit. Jenny slipped two $1 bills inside the purse with a note saying, "I hope you enjoy this lovely purse." Finally, someone bought it for the $1.50 asking price. Now, that's marketing!

Your Role in this Entrepreneurial Enterprise

By now you are probably wondering if there is a point to this story that has something to do with you. Yes, there is, and I was just coming to it.

Your official role in all of this is to be your wife's gofer – to go for whatever she tells you to go for. What you really should be doing, however, is guarding your own stuff. You see, in addition to getting into her closet and finding stuff that she doesn't wear any more, she has probably gotten into your closet and hauled out every piece of clothing that she has never liked, or that she deems no longer fits you, or you have not worn in the past two months.

You need to carefully scrutinize every single piece of merchandise that she has displayed for sale. You may be amazed to find that your old set of golf clubs, the bowling ball you haven't used in two years, several pair of your shoes, some of your pants, shirts, coats, and even socks and underwear have found their way onto the garage sale showroom.

How does your Grandfather know this? Experience, my good man, experience. Three years in a row I saved my prized black and white checkered sport coat from Grandma's garage sale. On her fourth sale, Grandma outmaneuvered me and now some extremely well-dressed guy is running around town wearing a beautiful black and white checkered sport coat. He's probably also wearing a lavender shirt with it, which also mysteriously disappeared from my closet. As you can imagine, an outfit like that is hard to replace.

The Garage Sale Cycle

Your wife will make hundreds of dollars from her garage sale and she will be hooked. What will she do with the money? Well, she will go shopping for blouses, jeans, coats, and shoes, which will eventually find their way onto the garage sale that she will hold two or three years from now. It's a vicious cycle, but it's a great way to make some easy money and you just gotta admire her for her entrepreneurial spirit. Cash.

Your wife's suggestions on what you should wear,

how you should hold your dinner fork,

how fast you should walk or eat,

how loud you should talk,

and opinions on other aspects of your daily life

should not be construed as criticism – it is "Training."

YOUR WIFE, THE ADDICT

This is a tough way for you to get the news, but someone has to tell you. Your wife will have a lifelong addiction that no power on earth, including you, will be able to cure. It is not booze or drugs – it is much more powerful than either of them. It is an urge to splurge.

Have you heard about women who own more than a hundred pair of shoes or have fifty purses or two hundred scarves? Well, it doesn't really matter if you have heard of those women or not because your wife has. They are her idols and her inspiration. She wants to be just like them so other women will look up to her and admire her because she has two hundred pair of shoes, a thousand hats, three hundred plastic pink flamingos, six hundred salt and pepper shakers in the shape of chickens, or four hundred rubber duckies. It is more than an addiction; it's a contest.

You are expecting advice on what to do about this addiction of your wife. Nothing. That's the advice – do nothing.

You see, she's ready for you if you start complaining about it. Her speech goes something like this, "I don't spend money on gambling, drinking, smoking, drugs, golf, bowling, soccer, or going to football games, basketball games, baseball games . . . ."

And, that's just the introduction of the speech before she gets into the main part. By the time she gets done, you're gonna be begging her to let you buy her a couple of pair of shoes or a purse or two for her collection. It's just not worth complaining about, young man.

How is your Grandfather so wise? Experience, my good man, experience. I have heard "The Speech" first hand, from Grandma, and it ain't pretty.

I repeat my aforementioned advice on how to handle your wife's lifelong addiction – *Nothing. Do Nothing.*

*"Buy me flowers, candy, jewelry, clothing,
perfume, a card,*

or nothing at all —

but do not ever buy me an implement of work as a gift."

HER SILENT, BUT VERY LOUD, LANGUAGE

Okay, talking about *Body Language* here – that silent language that is often louder and more powerful than a scream.

You have been aware of body language all of your life and you use it on a daily basis. Here's a little quiz: Identify what the following body language means. (Even though you probably don't need a solution to this little quiz, the answers are shown below.)

Scenario No. 1: Someone extends to you a closed fist with their thumb straight in the air, a smile on their face.

Scenario No. 2: Someone holds up their hand in front of you displaying a circle that they have formed with their thumb and index finger.

Scenario No. 3: You cut a driver off in traffic and he rolls down the window and extends his hand in your direction, with his fist clenched and his middle finger straight in the air.

Scenario No. 4: A man has been out carousing with his buddies for three nights in a row. His wife meets him at the door when he arrives home at 2 a.m., with a Bible in one hand and a cast iron skillet in the other.

Here are the answers:

Answer to Scenario No. 1: "Thumbs up; good going!"

Answer to Scenario No. 2: "A-Okay; You done good!"

Answer to Scenario No. 3: "Up yours."

Answer to Scenario No. 4: "One way or the other, the wife is determined to change this guy's behavior."

When your wife speaks to you, her body language may be more subtle and therefore far more difficult to interpret than

71

the examples shown above. To complicate things, there are hundreds of body parts and a small movement one way may mean one thing and a slight movement of the same body part another way might mean the exact opposite. Nevertheless, check out the following interpretations of common body language, which might be helpful in understanding what your wife is saying to you or, maybe, not saying.

Voice

If her voice is strong, powerful, and lively and if it has her normal tone, your wife is most likely happy, upbeat, and positive. You are a lucky man to have such a pleasant wife.

If her voice is halting or trembling or if her vocal tone is considerably lower or higher than normal, she may be feeling downhearted, distressed, sad, or may not be feeling well. Naturally, the first thought that pops into your head is, "What in the hell have I done now?" But, maybe it's not even you; it could be work related, the weather, or a misunderstanding with a friend or her mother. In other words, you have no idea, yet.

Silence

Researchers have determined that there are one hundred sixty-seven different reasons why a woman may be silent, some of which are good, some of which are bad, and some of which are neutral. Do not even try to figure it out, because you can't.

Eyes

If her eyes are bright and sparkling, and she is making eye contact with you, she is undoubtedly happy and excited. Making eye contact with you might also reflect that she is confident, truthful, and composed. What a gal, you lucky dog!

If her eyes are lifeless or if she looks down or looks from side to side, failing to make eye contact with you, she may be unhappy, troubled, or even untruthful. Did you do something to cause this? Probably. Now all you have to do is figure out what you did – this time.

If she rolls her eyes, it is clear that she does not believe a word you're saying, or maybe she thinks you're just beating the same old horse to death as in, "Here we go again." For example, I am even considering the possibility that maybe I should stop telling the story about my great-great-great-great-grandfather, Ferdinand Grillier, the full-blooded Frenchman, who was in Napoleon's army when they invaded Russia in 1812. Or at least, maybe I will leave out the part about how the Russian soldiers captured him and were going to kill him but then they decided to let him go because – wait for it - "Because he was such a handsome man." Grandma claims she has living proof that part of the story is not true. I wonder what she means by that.

Winking

A wink can be positive, negative, or flirtatious, depending upon what else is going on at the same time. It often means agreement or acceptance or is a way of saying, "You know what I mean."

Sometimes the most important thing about a wink is who the *winkee* is that the *winker* is winking at. For example, if you, Joel, a man, wink at a woman and your wife catches you, you may need to think quick to come up with an explanation that doesn't get you in deeper than you already are. And the old, "I had a speck of dust in my eye" has not worked since junior high school.

Head

If your wife nods her head up and down, it is a sign of agreement; if she shakes her head from side to side, it is a sign of disagreement or disbelief. If she says one thing with words but her head movement indicates the opposite, most likely the head movement is what she really means. Let's say that your wife is having cocktails with a couple of friends. The conversation naturally turns to their husbands. Your wife shakes her head from side to side and says, "My husband is just wonderful around the house; I don't even have to ask him to pitch in and help out – he does it on his own." What do you think her friends got out of that?

If her head is held high, it may be a sign that she is interested in what you are saying. If her head is down, she may be avoiding the issue at hand or may be in disagreement or be bored. Let's say you are giving her a blow by blow account of a training session that you were required to attend, that even you found boring. How high do you think your wife's head will be as she listens to your report?

Smile

If her smile involves her whole face, including her eyes and lips, it is probably a genuine smile. If only her lips are involved, it's probably a forced or fake smile. You have seen Abby smile during many happy times. You should be able to spot a fake or forced smile from across the room. That's the easy part. The hard part might be – why?

Lips

If her bottom lip sticks out or protrudes, it may be a sign that she is unhappy or pouting. If she bites her lip, it may be a sign of tension or nervousness. What in the hell have you done now?

Laugh

It is said that you can fake damn near anything, but you can't fake a laugh. Could be. Give it the mirror test and see if you can create a believable fake laugh. If you can, you may be in the wrong business – Hollywood or politics could use you.

Touching Face

Touching her face, with her fingers on one side and her thumb on the other side as she drags the hand downward towards her chin, can be a sign of contemplation or of being thoughtful. Maybe she repeats the motion several times, stroking her face.

No doubt, many a college professor or psychiatrist has practiced this in the mirror. You would be well advised to likewise practice this maneuver until you have it perfected. Then, you might contemplate changing professions.

Frying Pan

Frying Pan clenched in her fist, held high above her head as she charges at you. (Just checking if you're still with me.) Of course you would not do anything that would cause your wife to do this. But, if she does, run like hell. You can explain later.

Hands

If she holds a hand over her heart, she is showing her sincerity or is seeking to be believed.

If her fingers are tapping the tabletop, she may be nervous or anxious.

If your wife jabs a finger at you, it may be a sign of aggression or confrontation or it may be to simply emphasize a point in a non-threatening way. If she points and winks at the same time, it is probably a friendly sign of acknowledgment or a confirmation of "Right on."

If her fist is clenched, it may be a sign of great determination or, on the other hand, it might be a sign of aggression.

This discussion of what the movement and motion of your wife's hands and fingers might mean is quite interesting to you, we presume. However, in real life in real time, you have three-fifths of a second to process all of this and make a correct interpretation. Tick, Tick, Tick.

Arms

If her arms are crossed in front of her chest, she is probably feeling negative and is blocking out what you are saying, or worse yet, blocking you out.

Leaning

If she leans toward you as she talks to you, she is engaged, interested, focused, and comfortable with you. If she leans away from you, the opposite is probably true.

Of course, if you talk real low or whisper, you might be able to get her to lean in toward you to hear what you're saying. If your words are not captivating, this technique won't keep her engaged for long. Better to rely on a powerful and interesting message.

Touching

If she touches you lightly on your hand, arm, or shoulder as she speaks, she is strongly emphasizing her point in one of the most powerful non-threatening ways there is to drive home a message. It is a sign that she is into you and strongly wants your input or approval.

Years ago, this technique of touching someone on the arm or shoulder when delivering a message was taught by sales trainers as a way to magnify a message and drive it home. Today, it will get you sued for harassment, assault, or both. Better stick to using this technique on your wife, assuming she doesn't mind your touching her.

Space

If your wife sits close to you when she talks, it is a sign of warmth and that she is comfortable with you and engaged with you. If she maintains an unusual amount of space between you, that "Nothing" she said was wrong is actually "Something."

Consider Everything, and Then . . . .

So, there you have a small sampling of some normal interpretations of body language. As you can see, some of the same body movements or gestures can have widely varying interpretations, depending on other factors happening at the same time. Take her words, voice tone, facial expressions, and other body signs into consideration as you attempt to interpret what she is saying and what it actually might mean.

You will come to know your wife better than anyone on earth. As you do, you will come to know her own personal movements, gestures, and signs that indicate her personal body language that you, and you alone, will be able to interpret.

Well, let's be honest – some of the time you will be able to do this. The rest of the time you will do what every husband on earth does in trying to interpret his wife's moods, actions, movements, and gestures – *Consider everything, and then. . . .* GUESS!

In the meantime, here's a little practice for you – what do you think it means if your wife raises her eyebrows after you have made a comment that you believe was quite profound?

You're right! She thinks you're full of "It."

Becoming Even More Exemplatory

(EXEMPLATORY: Adj. – Exemplary, Meritorious)

This may be difficult for you to comprehend, but even as fabulous and wonderful you are, there may be a small amount of room for improvement – to become even more exemplatory than you already are. Perhaps you will pick up a pointer or two from the following.

UNPREDICTABLE YOU

What happens to a football team that always runs off left tackle on first down, always runs off right tackle on second down, and always passes on third down? The answer is - they punt on fourth down because they have become so predictable that their opponent knows what they're going to do before they do it and they stop them in their tracks. And, they are b-o-r-i-n-g.

Hey, Coach, how about shaking things up a bit and passing on first down, running a reverse, using a fleaflicker, or throwing in a fumblerooski now and then to become unpredictable – maybe even exciting.

Of course, we're not talking about football in this little metaphor - we're talking about you. Develop an exciting personal game plan so you do not become predictable and boring in your relationship with Abby - not now, not ten years from now, not twenty years from now, not ever. Continue to be the exciting, spontaneous, fun, slightly crazy guy that she fell in love with.

Surprise!

Why do people look forward to seeing what the prize is at the bottom of a Cracker Jack box? Why do people wrap presents rather than just handing over the unwrapped box? Why do people go along with it when someone says, "Close your eyes?" It's because everyone is thrilled by the surprise of the unknown.

Likewise, your wife will be thrilled if every once in a while you spring a little surprise on her. Maybe bring her flowers for no reason at all; she might especially appreciate them if they are wild flowers that you picked yourself. Volunteer to help with some household task that you normally don't get involved in. Surprise her with tickets to a concert or ballgame that you know she'd love to go to. Throw a surprise party for her birthday or to commemorate some milestone or accomplishment in her life.

Maybe you could arrange to have a long-lost friend of hers come to visit or maybe just call her on the phone. Why not take her on a surprise trip out of town for the night or over the weekend?

How about writing her a poem. It doesn't matter if it's well written or it's sophomoric – she'll love it from the bottom of her heart and will cherish it forever.

Why not give her a special, unexpected, gift. It can be large or small, costly or inexpensive – it doesn't matter, for it really is the thought that counts. And, while you're at it, why not give her the gift with a flair.

If it is a small item like a piece of jewelry, maybe you could put it in the bottom of a bag of popcorn that you give to her. Maybe you could place the gift in a small box inside a series of larger boxes that she has to open to get to it. Maybe you could have a mysterious package delivered to your door by a courier or delivery company. Perhaps you could blindfold her and lead her by the hand to the gift, where you whip off the blindfold and dazzle her, just like in the movies or in television commercials.

Maybe you could hide the gift somewhere in the house and then plant a series of notes that she has to follow to find it. Of all the gifts that you give her throughout your lifetime, the ones that you surprise her with will be among the most memorable for her and the ones that she will remember forever. Here is a true story:

The Ring He Could Not Afford to Not Afford

Shortly after Grandma and I were married, we spotted a beautiful, unique ring that was quite expensive in a jewelry store window. Grandma adored it but she didn't even ask if I would buy it for her since, just starting out, money was tight. We often passed by that jewelry store and we always stopped to admire the ring in the window.

One day, I stopped in to talk to the jewelry store owner and the owner said he'd sell the ring to me on layaway and I could pay him what I could whenever I could until it was paid for.

It took a while, but I finally got that ring paid for. I was bursting with pride and excitement as I hid the ring in the house and hid little notes, starting with one behind the sugar bowl in the cupboard, that would lead Grandma to the ring. I will never forget Grandma's surprise, sheer joy, excitement, and appreciation when she found the ring.

That was some decades ago. Since then, Grandma and I have been fortunate and I have purchased Grandma numerous rings including some very nice ones. Grandma wears those rings from time to time, but the one ring that she *always* wears is the one that she and I spotted in the jewelry store window those many years ago. It is a beautiful ring, yes, but to Grandma, the memory of my surprising her with it and what the ring represents is the most beautiful thing of all. You have seen that ring many times, Joel – it's the one she wears on the middle finger of her left hand, next to her wedding ring.

Don't Throw the Baby Out with the Bath Water*

Another time, I bought Grandma a nice gold ring inlaid with several different precious stones and I hid it in the bottom of a bag containing a sandwich. She ate the sandwich, crumpled up the bag and tossed it in the garbage. Fortunately, I was there to retrieve the bag. Learn from this, as I did - if you present a gift to Abby with a flair or some showmanship, make sure you're there to save the day in case your idea backfires. P.S. Joel, you never knew that Grandpa was such a romantic devil, huh!

*If you've never heard this saying, look it up. It's from an earlier era, and you'll be surprised!

Who's Having the Most Fun Here, Anyway!

The great thing about giving your wife a surprise is that it is so much fun to plan, organize, and spring on her - and it's just as much fun to watch her reaction. She will love it, guaranteed. And, your surprises for her will form a special bond between the two of you and will create moments that you will both cherish forever.

Besides that, it will be a great story that your wife will recount to friends and relatives dozens of times throughout the years – a true sign that your fabulous surprise and flamboyant presentation made a lasting impression on her.

*When your wife gives you that steely-eyed,
clinched-jaw scowl, known as "The Look,"
it means that you have obviously done
something wrong, but what?
You will find out as soon as she gets you alone.*

THE PERFECT GREETING CARD

There are several special times throughout the year when you will give Abby a greeting card for her birthday, Valentine's Day, your anniversary, or some other occasion.

The philosophy about giving greeting cards, the process of selecting the right card, and the method of presenting it to the recipient, vary widely from marriage to marriage and person to person. It is an interesting study in human motivation and behavior. Take a look at a few carefully chosen case studies.

The "Rocket Shopper"

Ace considers himself to be one of the fastest shoppers on the planet. He is capable, at least in his own mind, of flinging open the door to a store, storming in, selecting what he came for, paying for it, and exiting the store, all before the door he entered has even closed. That's fast, folks.

Being a *Rocket Shopper* has its advantages, for sure. Our friend, Ace, saves enough time with his speedy shopping to accomplish twice what a normal person can in a day.

Being a Rocket Shopper also has potential drawbacks. For instance, take the time that Ace roared into the card shop to buy a birthday card for his wife. He spotted a great-looking card from ten feet away as he approached the birthday card section. Ace gave the card a quick once-over and was on his way out of the store in less than one minute. True Rocket Shopping.

Ace scribbled his wife's name and "I Love You" on the inside of the card, signed it, and proudly presented it to his wife. Ace's wife opened the envelope with a big smile on her face, and was greeted with a card that said in bold glitter, "HAPPY BIRTHDAY – TO MY MOTHER."

Instead of the normal response of "Thank you for the lovely card," his wife's response to this card was, "You Dumb Shit."

Here's a little advice for all the Rocket Shopping Aces of the world: you can get by with something like this once, providing your wife has a reasonably good sense of humor, but from now on you're walking on eggshells. Take an extra minute and actually read the card before you buy it. You might be surprised by the wonderful things it is saying to your wife that you will get credit for.

In case you haven't figured it out, "Ace" was actually me, your Grandfather, and the foul-mouthed recipient of the card was your Grandmother.

The Happy Shopper

Andy loves his wife and eagerly looks forward to selecting just the right card for her birthday, anniversary, or Valentine's Day that delivers a meaningful message of everlasting love, gratitude, and commitment.

Andy reads every card in the store, looking for just the right one that will convey the feelings that are in his heart. There are so many well-written, beautiful cards that it is often difficult to pick the very best one.

One year, Andy narrowed his selection for an anniversary card down to two choices, both of which carried beautiful heartfelt messages. He couldn't decide which card to buy, until inspiration hit – why not buy both of them!

After reading both cards, Andy's wife broke down in tears. She will never forget that anniversary, she will keep the cards forever, and she will repeat the story a hundred times about how she received two anniversary cards from her wonderful, loving husband.

Joel, in this story, Romantic Andy is, once again, me, your Grandfather. I was trying to make up for the Rocket Shopper escapade described previously.

Happy, Happy Valentine's Day

Grandma and I have a unique Valentine's card ritual that we do every year.

On Valentine's Day, we go to a card shop together and carefully study the cards. After serious contemplation, we select a card for each other. We exchange cards on the spot and read the card carefully selected for us by each other. We thank each other for the wonderful, meaningful card and share a hug and a kiss right there in the card shop.

Then, we put the cards back on the rack and go to our favorite bar and buy some cocktails with the money we would have spent on the cards. And, that's how Grandma and I have a Happy, Happy Valentine's Day.

The World's Most Powerful Greeting Card

The preceding examples are presented to stimulate your imagination in selecting meaningful greeting cards for your wife, and in presenting them to her. The goal in selecting a greeting card is to find one that says exactly what you would say to your wife if you had written the card yourself.

Whoa, Nellie! Why not! Why not junk the idea of buying a card from a card shop and write the card yourself! But, you're not a writer, you say. Poor excuse – just write from your heart.

But, you don't know what words to use. If you're hinting that I should write a greeting card verse for you to plagiarize, that's not going to happen – you've got to write your own card for your own wife. But, I will give you some pointers, sample words and phrases, and examples that will get you started in the right direction.

But, what if you do such a lousy job that Abby will hate it and you'll make a fool of yourself. Well, you've heard the saying, "It's the thought that counts." This is probably the situation the guy who created the saying was thinking about. Your wife will absolutely adore it, even if your writing isn't anywhere near the standard of the writing in the store-bought cards. She will love it and every loving, meaningful, sincere word you write will hit her straight in the heart like a sledgehammer.

This is the one card that Abby will treasure above all others. She might even carry it in her purse the rest of her life and many years from now, when she passes on, she might even request that it be placed in the casket with her so it will be with her forever. It's that powerful.

You can do it and I will guide you to help you get started with my simple card-writing system described below.

Wonderful words for your greeting card: As promised, here are some words and phrases that you might work into your greeting card: "Dear," "Dearest," "Darling," "Love," "Love you," "Love of my life," "Lover," "Forever," "Best," "Best thing," "Ever," "Every," "Everything," "Can," "Cannot," "Nothing," "Always," "Happened," "With," "With you," "Without," "Without you," "Beside," "World," "In the world," "Me," "To me," "We," "Us," "You," "I," "My," "You are," "Will," "Will be," "When," "What," "Wonder," "Together," "Blessed," "Possible," "Fortunate," "Partner," "Soulmate," "Friend," "Wonderful," "Live," "Life," "Think," "Think of you," "Dreams," "Plans," "Above," "Beyond," "Inspiration," "Thank," "Thank you," "Being there," "Only," "Fly," "Soar," "Eagle," "Sun," "Sunshine," "Moon," "Moonshine," "Stars," "Universe," "High," "Higher," "Heart," "Soul," "Mind," "Head," "Hands," "Full," "Total," "Complete," "All," "The," "That," "Then," "Than," "This," "Is," "Are," "Am." You can add some to the list if you want, but these may be all the words you need.

Writing your message: Start your first sentence with one of these words, *The, You, My, I, When, We,* or any similar word that comes to mind. Then, string together some of the words and phrases from the above list until you have a loving sentence that will astound even yourself.

Here's an example: "My Darling, You are the Love of My Life. With you, everything is possible. I can fly like an eagle and soar above the moon with you beside me." (Please note: All of the words in this example are from the list above.)

How about a little practice before you write your greeting card for real. Using words from the list above, complete this sentence:

"You -."

Also complete this sentence:

"I - - - - - - - - - - - -- -."

See! It's not hard at all. Now, organize your thoughts, try to have a central thought or two, and write your greeting card message, and before you know it, you *is* an author.

All professional writers go back over their work and proofread, edit, and polish what they have written before it becomes the final draft. You should do likewise.

Your message will be great and Abby will love and cherish it forever. You'll see!

Creating your greeting card: Take a standard sheet of paper, measuring 8 1/2" by 11" and fold it so it resembles a greeting card. You might use colored paper.

Print a heading on the front of your card – something like, "HAPPY ANNIVERSARY TO ABBY, THE LOVE OF MY LIFE." Next, write or print your greeting card message on the inside of the card in your own handwriting.

You might consider drawing or sketching a meaningful object on the cover or inside of the card. So what if you're no Leonardo Picasso – Abby will love your drawing and, maybe, the worse it is the better she'll like it.

This is going to work and you will be forever grateful

that you did it because it will please your wife so very much, forever.

Your wife may not look it, but when she gets in a mall, she is very quick. If you turn your back on her for just two seconds, she will be gone, and you won't see her again for three or four hours.

EATING ETIQUETTE

This is not going to be a lecture about which hand to hold your fork and knife in, when to place your napkin on your lap, or the maximum number of peas to balance on your knife blade. You can rely on your wife to train you on those matters.

This is about a dining matter of far more significance to you than that, since you are a guy. Since you are a guy, you will rarely be able to eat a full meal without spilling something on yourself. You have probably already discovered this on your own.

Scientific Eating Etiquette Truisms

There are several unwritten hypothesis about spilling food on yourself that are as accurate as any known law of science:

- The more colorful the food item, the more likely it is to spill on you. Thus, there is a 100% chance that when you eat spaghetti, boom, the sauce will get you.
- A light-colored shirt, like white or yellow, will attract food at a 75% higher rate than a dark-colored shirt.
- The larger the number of people dining at the same table as you, the greater the chance you will spill on yourself. If you are dining alone, there is only an 11% chance you will spill. If three people are dining with you, it raises to 58%, and if there are seven or more people at your table, there is a 98.99 percent chance of a spill.
- The softer the food item, the greater the chance that it will hit the front of your shirt around nipple height and slide all the way down to your belly button, creating a

wider path the further it goes. This includes food items like over-easy eggs, pudding, and chocolate cake with gooey frosting a half inch thick.

- The harder the food item, the greater the number of times it will hit your clothes and the greater the number of clothing items it will hit as it bounces its way toward the floor. For instance, a strawberry that is dripping in juice will hit your shirt around your top button, hit your shirt another two times, hit the front of your pants twice, hit your pants leg three times, hit your sock once, and end up on top of your neighbor's shoe.

- If you are eating a food drenched in syrup or some other sticky substance, there is 100% chance you will spill it on the front of your shirt and it will run like a river toward your belt buckle. Not only that, but you will instinctively touch the front of your shirt with your hand to see if you have spilled, which you have, and your hand will now be sticky. About this time, your boss will approach your table and want to shake hands.

- As time goes on, you will undoubtedly develop new, creative, unimaginable ways to spill on yourself that no one in the history of mankind has ever discovered before. For instance, while drinking a cup of hot chocolate with those little marshmallows in the cup, you might tip the cup up for a drink and one of the marshmallows, partially melted by the hot chocolate, will slosh against your face and become attached to your nose. Immediately after you tip the cup back down, the little marshmallow will become unattached from your nose and plummet southward to land on your shirt, gooey side down, of course. Very creative.

- As soon as you feel a food item hit your shirt, you will instinctively shoot a quick glance at your wife to see if she has seen it. At least 100% of the time, if not more, your wife will see it before it even hits your shirt. There is a small amount of comfort in this for you, since it will give her adequate forewarning to position her legs and feet out of the path of any incoming missile. She is still going to be disgusted with you, but nothing like she would be if she were to take a direct hit.
- All the other guys at the table will sympathize with your plight, since they have been there before and will be there again.
- The other wives at the table will sympathize with your wife for being married to such a slob.
- For every decade that you get older, the likelihood of spilling on yourself when you eat, doubles.

Mopping the Sopping

To every problem there is a potential solution and that is what this tome is all about, helping you find solutions to your problems that will result in making you a better husband. So, here are my eating etiquette solutions:

- If at all possible, avoid eating in public where you are apt to make a fool of yourself by spilling all over yourself.
- If you are forced to eat in public, try to keep the number

of guests at your table as low as possible to decrease the number of witnesses.

- Consider ordering food items that barely leave a trace if they happen to find their way to your shirt. Un-buttered toast or crackers are suggested.
- If you know you are going to eat a particular meal that is of a particular color, wear a shirt of the very same color so the food will blend in when it hits you. For instance, if you're going to eat spaghetti, wear a red shirt. Genius, no?
- If you are invited to someone's house for dinner, where you do not know what will be served, wear a multi-colored shirt, which will prepare you for any food offering.
- Consider spraying all of your shirts with the same stuff they spray on cloth furniture so spills will not stain them.
- By this time, your wife has undoubtedly been threatening to buy you a bib to wear. You might give it some serious thought.
- As soon as you spill something, clasp your hand and arm to your chest to cover the point of attack and immediately jump up and run to the restroom. By now you should be experienced in using just the right mixture of water and soap on a paper towel to vigorously scrub the stains from your shirt, and also your pants, socks, and shoes, if necessary. Wait twenty minutes for your clothes to dry, and rejoin your wife and friends. Because of the amount of time involved in this procedure, it is practical to do

this only once in an evening.

- When you buy shirts, always buy two that are identical. When you go out to eat, wear one and keep the second shirt handy as a backup. If you spill on your shirt, quickly excuse yourself and change into the backup when no one is watching. If you subsequently also spill on the backup shirt it may be best to excuse yourself and to quietly go home. No one will blame you.

- These are all good, solid, practical solutions, you've got to admit. Perhaps the best solution to your problem of spilling food on yourself every time you eat, however, is this – you're a guy. Guys are supposed to go out with their wife and friends and have fun and eat and be merry. So, go ahead and order anything you want even if it's loaded with sauces and juices oozing all over the place. Dig in with both hands and enjoy yourself and let the chips fall where they may, along with the salsa, syrup, spaghetti sauce, mustard, ketchup, and anything else that feels more comfortable on your shirt than on your plate.

Bon Appetit!

Maybe your wife is a first-rate cook and housekeeper; maybe she's not. Even if she isn't, keep in mind that you didn't marry her for her domestic skills, anyway. You married her for her companionship and the love and joy that the two of you share.

CHIVALRY

Joel, that goofy look on your face right now apparently means that you have never before seen that word, *Chivalry*, have no idea how to pronounce it, and have no clue about what it means. It probably also means that you're a fairly normal guy for this day and age. But, I'm about to change all that.

Chivalry (pronounced "shiv-ul-ree") is the act of a man extending to a woman courteous, honorable, polite, respectful, attentive, gallant, and well-mannered behavior. A chivalrous man might even be thought of as being charming, polished, and dashing—something like your Grandpa, if I may say so myself.

The Chivalrous Man in Action

If walking down the sidewalk with a woman after it has rained, the chivalrous man will walk on the outside, along the street, so if water splashes from a passing vehicle, it will splash on him and not on her. If there is a water puddle in front of her on the sidewalk, he might remove his jacket and cover the puddle so his lady will not get her shoes wet. He will open doors for her, including the car door, and not only on the first date.

The chivalrous man will hold an umbrella for a woman and will offer his handkerchief if she gets a speck of dust or a tear in her eye. If it is chilly, he will whip off his coat to provide her with extra warmth. If it is hot, he will offer her a cool drink.

The chivalrous man will pull out a woman's chair to seat her at a restaurant. If he knows what she prefers to drink, he will order it for her. If she goes to the restroom, he will stand when she rises from her chair and will again stand when she returns. If another female approaches their table, he will stand to greet her.

The chivalrous man will give small, but meaningful, gifts to his special woman for any reason or no reason at all. He will call her during the day just to say hello. He might read to her from a book of poetry or from a book of inspirational quotations. Perhaps he will write a poem just for his lady or he will handcraft a greeting card for her. If he possesses the chops, he might sing her a song or play her a tune on a musical instrument.

The Chivalrous man might even learn to say "I love you" in French ("Je Vous aime"), Italian ("Ti amo"), German ("Ich liebe dich"), or Swahili ("Nakupenda").

Chivalrous You!

Right now, you might be thinking that compared to the chivalrous character described in the preceding paragraphs, you are a social and cultural barbarian. There may be some truth in this, but, don't sell yourself short. There are dozens of ways in which you can display the courteous, polite, respectful, attentive, gallant, charming, polished, and dashing side of you to the woman you love.

Perhaps throwing your jacket over a mud puddle for Abby to walk on may be going a little bit too far, and your wife might even think you should have your mental state examined for doing it. Many of the other ideas are well within your capabilities, however. In fact, if you think about it, you are probably already doing some of these things on a regular basis. Keep up the good work, you *Chivalrous Devil,* you.

And, if ever in doubt how to handle a certain situation with chivalry and aplomb, you might ask yourself, "What would *Grandpa* do?" Ha!

*In interpreting what your wife's body language means,
carefully scrutinize her voice, eyes, head movement,
lips, laugh, fingers, hands, arms, and silence,
and then....Guess.*

KEEPING YOUR IN-LAWS FROM BECOMING OUT-LAWS

You are, most likely, the guy that your wife's mother warned her about when she first started dating – and now she has gone and married you. Besides that, her brother might wish she had married his best friend who she dated in high school and her dad was hoping she'd marry the banker's son.

Perhaps this is not the most ideal situation from which to launch a warm and fuzzy relationship with your in-laws, so you may have some work to do.

In-Law Philosophy 101

Here is a little homespun philosophy for getting along with your in-laws:

- Marrying into a family is similar to living in northern Minnesota in the wintertime, where there is snow on the ground from October to April, the temperature is routinely below zero, and ice is three feet thick on the lakes. You can sit around and complain about how miserable the winter is, or you can embrace it and get out and enjoy all that the winter has to offer.

  Interpretation: Embrace her family and become a bona fide part of it rather than sitting around and complaining about what a miserable bunch they are. Even if they are a miserable bunch, you'll probably only see them a few times a year, so think positive and make the best of it.

- Realize that your wife's parents, siblings, and other relatives are most likely very important to her. They are where she came from and she is an extension of them. So, if you find fault with them, you are, in essence, also finding fault with your wife. For instance, if you call her mother a bitch, you are indirectly also calling your wife a bitch, and now you're going to have two bitches mad at you.

- Do not even consider borrowing money from any of your in-laws, even if they suggest it. If, by some miracle, that which you borrowed money to invest in becomes a success, they will never let you forget that without their help this would have never happened. Worse yet, if you are unable to repay the money, it will only prove to them that you are the loser that they always suspected.

Congratulations, you not only have a new wife but you also have a new family. Give it a chance—who knows, maybe they'll even come to like you, eventually.

*It is not your fault that you spill on yourself
when you eat - it's hereditary. Your great-grandfather
did it, your grandfather did it, your father did it,
and now it's your turn.
Forewarn your sons what is ahead of them.*

THE WIND BENEATH HER WINGS

There are numerous things that you like, admire, and enjoy about your wife, or you wouldn't have asked her to marry you. Now that you're married, look for every opportunity to give her well-deserved compliments on her appearance, accomplishments, ideas, thoughtfulness, resourcefulness, perseverance, or anything else that stands out. She will appreciate your thoughtfulness and it will inspire her to continue with her winning ways.

Encourage Abby to pursue her goals and to follow her dreams and help her attain them in any way that you can. Be the wind beneath her wings that helps her soar like an eagle to greater heights than she ever imagined she could reach.

Deborah's Story

Years ago, a Regional Manager for a life insurance company asked me if I knew of anyone in the community who might make a good life insurance salesman for him to recruit. I said, "There's a young man, Charlie, fixing tires down at the Tire Store who seems to have a lot on the ball; you might talk to him."

Selling life insurance sounded good to Charlie, he got licensed, and within six months, Charlie was the top salesman in the region. In his spare time, Charlie read books on sales procedures and listened to motivational training materials. His excitement and enthusiasm was contagious and soon his wife, Deborah, got interested in sales.

"Do you think I can do it?" she asked her husband.

"I know you can," Charlie replied.

"What if I fail?" Deborah asked.

"If you fall, I'll be there to catch you," Charlie said. "Give it a try."

Deborah checked the local newspaper and saw an advertisement from a nationally-known cosmetic company that makes in-home sales by individual sales representatives.

Deborah applied for the job, got it, went through a short sales training program, and started selling. Within two months, Deborah was the top salesperson in her region.

Within eight months, Deborah was asked if she would take the position of Regional Sales Manager.

"Do you think I can do it?" she asked her husband.

"I know you can," Charlie replied.

"What if I fail?" Deborah asked.

"If you fall, I'll be there to catch you," Charlie said. "Give it a try."

Deborah was a natural as Regional Sales Manager and two years later was asked if she would take the position of State Sales Manager. Deborah didn't even have to ask her husband if she could do it; she knew that she could and she knew he would support her.

After a few years as State Sales Manager, Deborah was promoted to National Sales Manager.

Deborah did the work and earned her success and her promotions. Her husband, Charlie, also deserves some credit – for encouraging and supporting her, and then getting out of her way.

This is a true story and I am proud that I had a small role in it by recommending to the life insurance Regional Manager that he talk to Charlie down at the Tire Store.

Cindy's Story

Demonstrate your encouragement, support, and admiration for your wife's efforts and accomplishments in ways that go beyond words, as Cindy did in the following true story.

For nearly three years, Cindy's husband, Henry, got up two hours before her every day to work on writing a book. He finished it, but it took another year to land a literary agent who would represent it, another six months for the agent to find a publisher, and almost another year before the book hit the market. When the book finally came out, Cindy threw a surprise "Author's Book Release Party" for Henry. Cindy's surprise party is a lifetime highlight that Henry will always appreciate and will never forget.

Actually, this story is not about some fictitious "Henry" and "Cindy." It is the true story of me (aka Henry) and Grandma (aka Cindy) and that surprise party was about the coolest thing Grandma ever did for me. What a blast!

The Town Crier

Abby may be modest and may not divulge much about her accomplishments to her friends or even to her family. Here is where you come in – no one will blame you for being proud of your wife and for sharing what she has done.

In It for the Long Haul

British statesman, Winston Churchill, was an eloquent speaker who produced many sayings that are as true today as when he spoke them some seventy-five years ago.

One of his most famous quotes is appropriate for the relationship between you and your wife and for your marriage. In essence, Winston Churchill said, "Never give up, never give up; never, never, never, never quit."

Sure, you and Abby may face some difficult times through the years, but that's normal. That's life. If you follow Winston Churchill's adage, you and your wife will always find a way to work your way through it.

Since you and Abby are in it for the long haul, you may as well make some long-range plans. How about buying a home! How about becoming rich! How about surviving those inevitable spats that occur in marriages! How about fostering a supportive and loving marriage!

THE FABULOUS DREAM – OWNING YOUR FIRST HOME

At some point, Abby and you will probably get the idea that you should buy your own home. This idea could evolve naturally on its own, but the thought often intensifies shortly after your wife's sister and her husband or some good friends buy their first home. You and Abby look at each other and say, "Why not us?" And the idea is born.

There are several types of homes available for you to buy including a house, condominium, cooperative, town home, or duplex. The process of searching for a home and of buying it are basically the same for each of these.

Real Estate Speak

Let's assume close friends of yours recommend the real estate agent that they worked with, Claude, and you give him a call. He is eager to help you find the home of your dreams. Abby and you meet with Claude in his office, describe your needs and interests, and Claude selects some homes to show you that seem to be a good fit.

You and Abby pile into Claude's plush new Cadillac and you're off to find your dream home.

Claude really seems to know his stuff as he explains each home's many features and amenities: "This house is in a well-established neighborhood." "This is a prestigious new development." "My, what a cozy kitchen." "Isn't this winding staircase beautiful!" "What a comfortable den for watching TV or reading the newspaper." "This house has one magnificent full bathroom and one handy half bathroom." "You'll have a lot of fun in this fully-paneled basement." "You can put a lot of lawn and garden equipment in the spacious 6' by 10' storage shed in the back yard."

Interpreting Real Estate Speak

Be aware that the real estate profession has a language all

its own. The real estate agent, Claude in your case, describes the homes' features in accurate terms, but the customer, you, has the responsibility to interpret what each of those descriptions mean.

Here are a few examples of what Claude's glowing descriptions actually mean:

A house in an "established neighborhood" may mean the neighborhood is old, may be run down, and that therefore property values could easily decline in the future.

A house in a "new development" means that there are probably no trees and there will be more homes built in the neighborhood in the future and you will have no control over how large or small or goofy-looking they might be.

"A 'cozy kitchen' means that it might be large enough for Abby and you to eat in, but if you ever have guests it's too small for everyone, so someone will have to eat off of TV trays in the living room.

The "winding staircase" probably means you won't be able to haul furniture up it because of the twists and turns and you'll need to bring the furniture in through an upstairs bedroom window.

A "comfortable den" means this was once a bedroom that was too small to be a bedroom so they use it as a den.

A "full bathroom and a half bathroom" means that only one bathroom has a shower, so if you have guests or later on have a family, everyone will have to use the full bathroom to shower.

"A fully-paneled basement" might mean that the block

walls were caving in and they hid them behind the paneling.

Well, you probably get the idea. Just to check and see, though, what do you think it means when your real estate agent, Claude, said, "There is a spacious 6' by 10' storage shed in the back yard!" (Interpretation shown below – don't peek)

Notice, by the way, that it isn't just a 6' by 10' storage shed; it's a *spacious* 6' by 10' storage shed. When you studied English in school, you may not have understood the power of *adjectives*, but you're probably seeing it more clearly now. Did you notice that as Claude described each home's features and amenities, he sprinkled adjectives all over the place.

Well, here's the interpretation: Having a "storage shed" in the back yard probably means that the garage is too dinky to hold anything but a car or two and you need a shed to hold the rest of your stuff. Did you get it right?

Selecting a Home to Buy

There are numerous books on the market that contain valuable information on what to do and not do when selecting a home to buy. I suggest that you read them. I have only two suggestions for you, one of which is not contained in any of the books that I previously suggested.

Suggestion Number One: Sure, you'd like a house on the lake with a pool, hot tub, five bedrooms, six bathrooms, gourmet kitchen, formal dining room that will seat thirty, movie theater, bowling alley, eight stall garage, and guest house. There is only one rule here: *If you've got the money, go for it!* But if you don't have the money, don't fool yourself.

The second most miserable feeling on earth is becoming a slave to a home that you cannot afford, where virtually all of your money goes for the mortgage payment, real estate taxes, and insurance payments, leaving little money for anything else.

The single most miserable feeling on earth is when the bank repossesses your home because you cannot make the payments and you face the humiliation of your ass being kicked out on the street.

Start small. Buy something you can easily afford and work your way up to that dream home on the lake or ocean over time. You'll be very happy that you did. Every book giving advice on buying a home will tell you this, but it is so important that I wanted to restate it since, by now, you have no doubt come to trust my advice.

Suggestion Number Two: This advice is worth several thousand times the price you would pay for any book on how to buy a home – it's that valuable.

DO NOT buy a home that does not have your wife's full, complete, one hundred percent approval. If you insist on buying a house that she doesn't like or want or if you even try to subtly influence her decision, you will pay for it every day that you live in that house, and we're not talking about money. And, know what – you'll deserve your punishment because you ignored my sound advice.

When you're looking at a home and Abby says something like "This kitchen is awfully small," "There aren't many cupboards in the kitchen," "There isn't much closet space,"

"I would hate having to do laundry down in the basement," "There's not much storage space," "These bedrooms are awfully tiny," or "This is a crummy neighborhood," cross this place off your list. Immediately.

I repeat, DO NOT buy a home that your wife isn't absolutely crazy about.

There is one small variation to Suggestion Number Two above: If your wife, or you, are not crazy about the color of a couple of walls or the carpet in a room or two - that's cosmetic. You can easily take care of that before you move in. But, make sure you do in fact do it before you move in or it will be left undone for the entire time you live in the house. You will eventually paint that ugly wall or replace that horrible carpet, though. Know when? When you decide to sell the house and you realize that no one in their right mind will buy the house with that ugly colored wall and that horrible carpet.

Moving In – the 80-20 Rule

First, a little quiz – then we'll talk about the *80-20 Rule*. When you were a child, where did your family go for Thanksgiving dinner? *Grandma's House*. Where did you go for Christmas dinner? *Grandma's House*. Where did your mother grow up? *Grandma's House*. Where did your father grow up? *Your other Grandma's House*. Do you detect a pattern here? It's *Grandma's House* – not *Grandpa's House* and not *Grandma's and Grandpa's House* – its *Grandma's House*. So it shall be with the home that you and Abby buy. Your name may be on the deed along with your wife's, but for all practical purposes, it is

Your Wife's House. It is important that you comprehend this, since it will help you to also understand and accept the *80-20 Rule.*

Simply put, your wife is in charge of 80% of the house and you're in charge of 20%. Let's start with the bedroom closet. Since your wife owns several times more clothing and pairs of shoes than you, it makes perfect sense that an 80/20 split of the closet space is fair, with her getting 80% and you getting 20%.

Your wife is also in charge of the dressers in the bedroom. The same 80/20 split that applies to the closet also applies to the dressers, except for one small modification.

Say there are two dressers in the bedroom with a total of ten dresser drawers. According to the 80/20 rule, your wife should get eight of the dresser drawers and you should get two of them. Here's where the modification to the 80/20 rule comes in - you will need to give up one of your dresser drawers since your wife has too much stuff to fit into her 80%. This will leave you with one dresser drawer, which is all that you need anyway for your socks and underwear. Do not complain about this seeming inequality of dresser drawer space or you might end up losing half of the one drawer that has been allotted to you. Know when you're well off.

Fine Tuning the 80-20 Rule

Since this is *Your Wife's House,* she is in charge of the kitchen, dining room, living room, laundry room, all bedrooms, all closets, and all hallways. Here is where the

80/20 rule gets a little tricky. The rooms that your wife is in charge of amount to roughly 80% of the space in the house, but she is in charge of 100% of that 80%. You may need to read that a couple of times to fully comprehend the concept. In simpler language, when it comes to decorating those rooms or arranging furniture in them, just stay the hell out of it and do as you're told.

Cheer Up – 20 is Better Than 0

At this point you may be feeling sorry for yourself, having just purchased and moved into a home where you are beginning to feel more like a guest than a permanent resident. Cheer up. We have not yet gotten to the part of the house that is your domain, your 20% – the garage.

Yes, you are in charge of the garage and you can do damn near anything that you want in it. In the garage, you are the king.

You can finish off the walls and paint them if you want to. You can even put in bigger light bulbs and can put up shelves or build a storage cabinet or two. You can put up a dart board and get yourself a radio to listen to while you throw darts. You might even buy an old refrigerator and fill it with beer and get a table and a few folding chairs so you and your buddies can sit out there in the garage and have a ball.

One word of caution, with all of this control and freedom to do what you want in the garage, don't forget to leave room for the car.

If your new home has a basement, you also may be able to

stake a claim to part of that as well, particularly if there is an unfinished area that you can use as a workroom.

If the basement has been finished off into a recreation room, with paneled walls, a finished ceiling, carpeting, and furniture, it is considered part of the house and is therefore under your wife's control. If, however, there is an area with a pool table, that rightfully should be considered part of your domain, even if it exceeds your 20%. Some of these territorial issues about who controls what are very complicated and may require negotiation and compromise. Do not get greedy with this or you may find yourself spending more time in the garage than you ever imagined.

Enjoy your new home, and may you joyfully co-exist there with your wife. Just remember who is in control of what and don't push your luck.

A married couple develops their own language and secret code. It might be a touch, wink, sigh, voice inflection, or word, such as "sleeo," that has special meaning to them. It is one of the unique things about married life that forms a special bond between the couple.

YOU'RE GOING TO BE RICH, RICH, RICH!!

I have good news for you; you're going to be rich. I will describe exactly how to do it and all you have to do is follow the simple system that I describe. But first, I want to pound some sense into your thick head.

You are not going to win the lottery, so give up trying. There is no long-lost uncle who is worth billions who is going to leave you a bundle in his will. You are not going to hit the Mega Millions jackpot in Las Vegas or go on a twenty-hour winning streak at the craps table – you'll be lucky to return home with gas money.

You are not going to magically record a multi-million selling song or write a bestseller book. Your wife's father may or may not be loaded, but it doesn't matter - he's planning on living to be a hundred. You are not going to buy $100 of stock in a start-up company that will become the next big thing that makes you a multi-millionaire overnight. It will happen – to someone else - but not you.

You are not going to find a twenty-pound gold nugget while hiking through the woods, and you're not going to find a bag of money in the ditch. You're not going to sign a multi-million dollar professional sports contract, but you already knew that. And, finally, you are not going to invent a product or technology that changes the world and makes you a kazillionaire.

In other words, you're too darned unlucky to get rich quick, so don't spend all your time daydreaming about it and don't squander your money chasing after it.

Before I divulge the secret that will make you rich, I am going to describe some money pits to avoid.

Investing in Stocks

There are thousands of companies in which you can buy part ownership in the form of common stock. Some of these companies are household names like General Motors, Apple, and Google. Others are small start-up companies operating on a shoestring out of a garage or storage building. There are several problems with investing in common stocks of individual companies.

Problem Number One: The prices of stocks go up and down on a daily basis like a yo-yo because of news reports about the economy, interest rates, politics, the weather, foreign countries, or dozens of other things.

Investors are a bunch of chickenshits who live and die on each day's news. If there's good news, they buy stocks like crazy and prices go up. If there's bad news, they panic and sell - and prices drop like a lead-filled balloon.

If investors would stop reading newspapers, stop listening to the radio, and stop watching television, they wouldn't jump in and out of the market like a bunch of scared chickens and everything would work out just fine. But, they don't, and they totally screw up the market.

Problem Number Two: Sorry to be the one to tell you this, but you are not astute enough to pick the right companies to invest in and not lucky enough to know when to jump in and when to get out.

Problem Number Three: You are a nice guy, so don't take this personally, but besides being uninformed when it comes to investing, you are also gullible, most likely. Let's say out of the blue, you receive an internet *HOT TIP* about a company where you can get in on the ground floor and it's going to go nuts. Why, it was selling for 10 cents a share just a month ago and it's already up to $5.00 a share and it's going up like a rocket. Jump in now the newsletter says – NOW!

Most likely, you are skeptical and a little scared, so you don't jump in right away when the stock is at $5 a share. You watch it climb to $6, then $7, then $8, then $9, and finally you can't take it anymore and you jump in at $10 a share.

Very likely, you will become the victim of a "Pump and Dump" scheme perpetrated by the guy sending you the "hot tip." It works like this – he bought a million shares when it was at 10 cents a share. Then, he started pumping the stock up with his "hot tip" newsletter and investors started to jump in, which is driving the price up. When the price gets high enough, say $10 a share, he'll dump his shares and make a bundle. Then, the price of the stock will drop like a rock and end up where it belongs based on the value of the company – around 10 cents a share.

Recall that you bought in when the stock was at $10 a share, and when the price started dropping you held on hoping it would go back up. Finally, when it hits 10 cents a share, you sell. You can calculate your loss by multiplying the number of shares you bought times your loss per share of $9.90.

If this little story scared the hell out of you, good. It will save you a lot of misery, and a lot of money. Please Note: Time for an embarrassing confession – that was ME in this example and I'd sure like to get my hands on that guy with his *Hot Tip*.

My Advice: Stay away from investing in common stocks of individual companies, for Reasons One, Two, and Three stated above.

Investing in Bonds

We'll make this short. There are a lot of investments, like government bonds, corporate bonds, municipal bonds, treasury bills, and money market certificates that pay interest on your investment.

My Advice: Normally, the interest rate is too low for a young person to invest in these. Four or five decades from now, when you want to be more conservative with your investments, you might consider it.

Investing in Commodities

This is certain to happen, so pay attention. Some day, a friend is going to say to you, "I know how we can make a killing in the commodities market – thousands of dollars a day." That is why I am giving you a little background knowledge here, so you will know what he's talking about.

Various commodities including sugar, coffee, lumber, corn, soybeans, wheat, cattle, hogs, and silver are traded on the Board of Trade. These commodities are traded in units called "contracts." For instance, a corn contract consists of

5,000 bushels.

Let's say that corn is currently selling at $5 a bushel, so a contract of 5,000 bushels is worth $25,000. Now, here is what might seem to make investing in commodities attractive – to buy, or control a 5,000 bushel contract of corn, you only need to put up 10% of the contract's $25,000 value, called a *Margin*. So, for $2,500 cash, you can control $25,000 worth of corn. You don't actually have to take delivery of the corn; you can sell your corn contract before it comes to that.

Let's assume that the price of corn goes up 20 cents the first day you own a contract. That's an increase of $1,000 (5,000 bushels x $.20 per bushel) in one day on your $2,500 investment! This amounts to an annual rate of return on your investment of a whopping 14,600%. Wow!!! You da investment guru, no? No.

Here's the killer. The price of corn can go down as well as up, and it can go down a whole lot faster than it will go up. Let's say there is a news report that the corn crop in Brazil is going to be double what was expected. Therefore, since the worldwide supply of corn is going to be larger than expected, the price of corn will drop like a falling meteorite.

Let's say corn drops $1 a bushel over a four-day period. Thus, you would lose $5,000 in one week on your 5,000 bushel contract of corn. That's bad, but the really bad news is that you and your pal each bought ten contracts of corn in your quest to get rich quick – your loss is $50,000 for the week. How did that feel?

My Advice: If you don't pay attention to any other advice

I'm giving in this epistle, pay attention to this. It might save you from bankruptcy and might save your marriage. DO NOT UNDER ANY CIRCUMSTANCES INVEST IN COMMODITIES. Got it?

Investing in Mutual Funds

A *Mutual Fund* is a company that pools hundreds of millions or billions of dollars from thousands of individual investors.

The Mutual Fund uses that money to buy shares of common stock, or other investments, in maybe 50-100 different companies. There are hundreds of different Mutual Funds, each designed to invest in certain types of companies to meet certain investment goals. For instance, a Mutual Fund might invest in the automotive industry or in pharmaceuticals or in retailers. Other Mutual Funds might invest in oil companies, mining, or computer manufacturers. Many mutual funds diversify by investing in a wide range of different types of companies.

When you invest in a Mutual Fund, you receive shares of the Mutual Fund, which, in essence, means your money is spread across the 50-100 companies the Mutual Fund invests in. Gone is the problem of trying to pick one or two companies to invest your money in.

Dollar Cost Averaging: One of the main problems of investing in the stock market is buying at the right time. *Dollar Cost Averaging* is an investment strategy that eliminates this problem. Simply stated, you would invest the same amount of money in a Mutual Fund every month on a regular basis. Sometimes you would buy at a low price, sometimes at a high price, and sometimes in between. Overall, your average purchase price would be a comfortable average somewhere in the middle.

With many Mutual Funds, you can start with an initial investment as low as $100-$500 and you can put in as little as $50 or $100 a month.

My Advice: I have just described to you how to become rich. Start now, investing in a Mutual Fund using Dollar Cost Averaging. Invest a comfortable amount each month by having it automatically transferred from your bank account to the Mutual Fund. Increase your monthly investment over time and invest in several different Mutual Funds as time goes on.

You will not become rich overnight, but as I described at the beginning of this section, that's just not in the cards for you. But, if you stick to your Mutual Fund investment program month after month, year after year, you will become Rich, Rich, Rich beyond what you ever thought possible. As promised - simple and fool-proof.

You, the Investment Guru

Now that you are the man with the plan, there is one more thing to do before putting the plan into action. You're married, remember? Well, investing for the future of you and Abby is something you should do together.

Dazzle Abby with your new found knowledge of

investing. No doubt she will be dutifully impressed and will follow your lead on the investment plan. Then, the two of you can share the journey and the results together. Even her father will wonder what in the hell came over you.

When it comes to buying that mansion on the lake,
that 32-foot cabin cruiser, or that fancy sports car,
there is only one rule:
If you've got the money, go for it!
If you don't have the money, don't fool yourself.

"IN THIS CORNER, WEIGHING IN AT . . . ."

True story. John and Martha have been married for over thirty-two years and they swear that in all that time they have never had even one disagreement, dispute, argument, spat, or fight. What's wrong with these people?

When two normal, decent, honorable, kind, considerate, loving people live together in close proximity day after day, like a husband and wife, there are bound to be times when there is some friction and there are issues. That's normal.

Here are some ideas that you can use to calm the troubled waters and to help you and Abby weather those marital storms.

Hear, Hear

When God created man, He gave him two ears and one mouth for a reason – that he should listen twice as much as he talks. We have it on good authority that He was specifically thinking of married men when He did this.

When Abby talks, listen intently so you do not misunderstand or misinterpret what she is trying to tell you.

The way in which your wife delivers her message is often more important and more powerful than the words that she says. Her delivery can either enhance the message relayed by her words, or it can contradict it. In fact, some communication experts say that up to seventy-five percent of the impact of a person's message comes from how it is delivered.

As your wife speaks, listen to the words she says, be aware of what she doesn't say, and weigh the tone of her voice and her body language.

One man seems to have learned this the hard way as evidenced by the wording of a classified ad he placed in the newspaper: "Boat For Sale – Apparently I misunderstood my wife when she said, 'Do what you want.'"

After You, Dear

Here is a little technique that will help you avoid some arguments and help you win others. When you and Abby have an issue with something, you will both be eager to state your case to support your position.

Keep your mouth shut and let your wife go first. Maybe what she says will make perfect sense to you and you'll agree with her and that will be the end of it. Maybe by talking it out, your wife will change her position. Maybe by letting her go first, she will reveal something to you that will be valuable for you to know.

This is based on a true story: Susan and Dan were in their early thirties and had been dating for over two years. Susan called Dan on a Wednesday afternoon and asked him to meet her at Pasquale's at seven for dinner because she wanted to talk to him about something.

Susan got to the restaurant first and Dan soon joined her. Susan said, "I would like to talk to you about something. I think . . ."

Dan interrupted her, "Susan, I want to say something first. We have been dating for over two years and although we get along great and have a wonderful time together, we don't seem to be going anywhere. I think it is time we go our separate ways."

Susan is stunned. "You mean it's over?"

Dan says, "It's over. I'm sorry."

"That's your final answer – there's nothing I can do to change your mind?" Susan asks.

"I'm sorry, but it's over," Dan says. "By the way, what was it you wanted to talk to me about tonight?"

"My uncle, Robert, who invented a component for computer processors, passed away and I inherited over twenty million dollars from his estate. Tonight I was going to ask you to marry me. Goodbye, Dan."

When "Nothing" Means "Something"

Here is a real-life example for you to evaluate. It is evening. You are sitting in your favorite chair in the living room reading the newspaper and Abby is in the kitchen. The pots, pans, and kettles seem to be rattling and clanking a little louder than normal and the cupboard doors seem to be getting slammed shut with authority. You, being in tune with body language and unspoken messages, sense that something is wrong.

You rise from your chair and approach Abby in the kitchen. "What's wrong?" you ask, trying to keep your voice calm and even.

"Nothing," she replies.

Even though she said the word, "Nothing," her tone of voice and overall appearance seem to say, "Something."

You quickly search your mind for a clue – what in the hell

have you done now or what did you say that irritated her? You can't put your finger on anything that you have done recently that should have upset her. But, there is "something;" there's no doubt about that.

This little scenario has been repeated in real life, word-for-word, billions of times between husbands and wives all over the globe. And, just like those billions of other husbands, you'd have a better chance solving Rubik's Cube blindfolded than coming up with a surefire method for determining what is bothering her. Basically, you have two options.

Option Number One: You can question, probe, and pry until you dig it out of her, which may or may not work.

Option Number Two: You can simply let it lie, figuring that she will eventually tell you when, and if, she's good and ready.

Either of these two techniques are fraught with potential advantages and pitfalls, but if we were to pick one, we'd suggest that you just let it ride until she's ready to bring it up on her own. It's wishful thinking, but maybe her somber mood has nothing to do with you and she'll work it out on her own.

Let the Tornado Blow

Not all women are wired this way, but it appears that many are. Every now and then, when the tension, stress, turmoil, and burdens of everyday life become too much to bear, they blow a gasket.

Your wife might rant, rave, and storm around the house for a while and even throw in a few swear words for good measure, just to make sure you understand how damn overwhelmed and unhappy she is.

Just follow the advice given by the weatherman on the radio when a tornado is spotted – take cover. When the storm is over, perhaps you can calmly comfort your wife and the two of you can work through her concerns together.

Win-Lose, Lose-Lose, and Win-Win Strategies

There are three different strategies that a person can choose from when they get embroiled in a controversy with someone else:

Win-Lose Strategy: In a win-lose strategy, a person's goal is not only that they win, but that their opponent ends up being stomped into the ground and totally devastated.

This is a poor strategy for anyone to use in an argument with one's spouse, since it only drives a permanent wedge between them.

Lose-Lose Strategy: In a lose-lose strategy, a person doesn't care what happens to themself as long as they bring down the other person. This arises from a situation filled with bitterness, hate, and vindictiveness. Nobody wins. What good is that?

Win-Win Strategy: In a win-win strategy, each person tries to find a solution where both parties come out of it feeling they have gotten something positive and good out of the deal. The result is good feelings all around and there is a solid foundation that has been laid for the future.

For example, maybe you would love to go to a basketball

game with a couple of friends on Saturday, but this would leave your wife home alone while you're out having fun, which might upset her.

Hey, how about suggesting that Abby and her sister go shopping while you're at the game and you can all meet up for cocktails or dinner later. Everybody has a good time and everybody wins.

How to Win Every Argument

How do you "win" every argument? By *agreeing* with your wife and not getting into an argument in the first place.

Granted, this won't work if there are major differences of opinion on important issues. It will work, however, on issues of minor consequence that don't mean a damn to you one way or the other.

For example, you and your wife are at home watching television and she says, "Is it chilly in here?" Obviously, she thinks it is or she wouldn't have brought it up. Even if you think the temperature is fine, what would it hurt to agree with her and let her turn up the thermostat a degree or two. Hey, you're a guy and you can stand the heat.

Argument avoided. Enjoy the TV show. By the way, this little scenario happens about three times a week between Grandma and me. Whether she thinks it's too hot or too cold in the room, I agree. According to my calculations, I have avoided over 7,000 arguments with Grandma using this little technique. Hey, I'm a guy – if it's a little too hot or a little too cool, I can take it.

Thirteen Magical Words

Throughout your married life, you will say millions of words to your wife. Those words will have a profound impact on her attitude toward you and, thus, on your entire relationship with her and the level of happiness that you both experience in your marriage.

There are over 1,025,000 words in the English language. From all those words, I have selected *Thirteen Magical Words* for you to use that will virtually guarantee a happy and successful marriage.

"I LOVE YOU" - These are the three most powerful words that you can say to your wife. They are the three words that she wants to, and needs to, hear from you often. Make it a point to tell her every day, and more than once. Why not make it a habit to tell her, "I Love You," within the first fifteen minutes after you awake for the day and within the last fifteen minutes before you retire for the evening. What a great way to start and finish each day.

"THANK YOU" - Your wife will do numerous things for you virtually every day. Maybe it's routine things like cooking dinner, ironing your shirts, picking up something from the store, or turning down the volume on the television so you can concentrate on a project you're working on. Recognize her kindness, her actions, and her contributions to you and to your marriage by simply saying, "Thank you."

"I AM SORRY" - You are my grandson and I love you; nevertheless, I know that you are fully capable of being one of the biggest screw-ups on the planet.

When you do screw up, don't make alibis or lame excuses or, worse yet, tell lies that are apt to compound the situation. Own it. Simply admit that you messed up, take Abby in your arms, and tell her, "I am sorry."

A philosopher once put this concept in slightly different words that you might understand: "If you have screwed up and have to eat shit, don't nibble."

"YES, DEAR" - There undoubtedly will be many interactions with Abby through the years that won't make a difference to you one way or the other. At other times, Abby may ask for your opinion, but what she really wants is agreement with what she has already done or has planned to do. In those situations, and in numerous other circumstances that will come along in your day-to-day life, there are two magical words that you should use often: "Yes, Dear." And then just blow it off.

For example, Abby may ask, "Do you think this chair looks okay sitting over here in the corner?" You wisely answer, "Yes, Dear."

Abby moves the chair to the center of the room and says, "Or, do you think it looks better here?" Again, your appropriate answer is, "Yes, Dear." Oh, Oh – she moves the chair to the other side of the room and asks if you like it there. Of course, your answer is "--- ----" Good Going!

"WE, US, OUR" - When you were single, it was appropriate for you to say things like, "I bought a new TV," "I want what's best for me," and "My car needs new tires." You lived in an "I, ME, MY" world, and that was completely proper, since you were single.

Now, you are married and things have changed; you're part of a team. When a football coach tries to exhort his players to work like a team rather than a bunch of individuals, he often says something like, "There's no 'I' in TEAM." When you talk about plans, goals, activities, possessions, and whatever, think of Abby and you as a team and use the words "We," "Us," and "Our" whenever possible.

Working as a team, you and Abby will be able to accomplish much more than the two of you working as separate individuals. This is called *synergy* and is sometimes described mathematically as 1 + 1 = 3.

A Lifetime of Magic

The *Thirteen Magical Words* described above really are magical. They will help Abby and you keep your love alive and will foster a feeling of appreciation, understanding, and respect between the two of you.

Use these magical words often throughout your entire married life and see if you can add a few magical words of your own to the list.

The Magnificent You!

Joel, not long ago, you were the proverbial lump of coal, but with my profound advice, Abby's training, and the potential that was there all along, you are now shining like a diamond.

To keep its shine, a diamond needs to be polished regularly, so go back and read the profound advice in this book every now and then, don't skip out on any of Abby's training sessions, and continue being exactly what you are and who you are.

One of these days, you're going to overhear your wife talking about you to one of her friends or to her mother and her words will astound you:

"My husband, Joel, is beyond wonderful – he is *Magnificent.*"

Wow! What a guy!!

www.ingramcontent.com/pod-product-compliance
Lightning Source LLC
Chambersburg PA
CBHW071347170626
46811CB00003B/1026